WEDDING BELL BLUES

Relentless Series Book 2, a novella

JENNIFER LYNN CARY

The Crockett Chronicles

"This book is so good! If you like Christian Historical Fiction, you will love this book. It hooked me on the first page and I couldn't put it down." —Ann Ferri

"I was drawn in by the idea that this series chronicles the descendants of Davy Crockett written with the fictional imagination of a direct descendant. The time period and a glimpse of the Huguenots made for an interesting story. I am excited to read more." —Jennifer Berry

"Exciting and grabs your attention from the first page! You find yourself there! A must read!" —Nova Forrest

"Excellent story of the Crockets. I could not put it down. The characters touched my heart." —Mary Rima

Tales from the Hob Nob Annex Cafe

"This is a well-written book that hooks you on the first page. It's a very enjoyable read that makes you forget about all your troubles and step back in time."—Ann Ferri

"Being an Indiana gal myself, and having been through Kokomo many times, I easily got caught up in this story."—Novabelle

"Great book and easy to read. I liked this book very much."—Kindle Reader

"I loved reading this book! It had me intrigued from the first page, and as the stories began, I could hardly wait to turn the page to see what happened next! Love the mix of true facts mixed with some good, clean, fun fiction! Easy, quick read. I highly recommend this book!"—CatSmit

Relentless Heart

"This book was beautifully written and the best book I read so far this year."—Peggy Baldwin

"While I have read other retellings of Ruth's story, somehow having her character be Vietnamese in the middle of the Vietnam War was the most appropriate translation I have yet seen. "—Phyllis, Among the Reads

"This is a beautifully written story. It is full of emotions and you can feel every one of them. It hooks you on the first page and keeps you turning the pages to see what happens next. I hated to see this book end and can't wait to read the next book in this series. This is a book you don't want to miss."—Ann Ferri

"I felt as if Hien, the beautiful, brave Vietnamese heroine, was having tea with me while sharing parts of her life." —Ginny

"Hien's story helped bring alive the story of Ruth for me." —Ruth Sand

Published by Tandem Services Press

Post Office Box 220

Yucaipa, California

www.TandemServicesInk.com

Scripture taken from the King James Version. In 1604, King James I of England authorized that a new translation of the Bible into English be started. It was finished in 1611, just 85 years after the first translation of the New Testament into English appeared (Tyndale, 1526). The Authorized Version, or King James Version, quickly became the standard for English-speaking Protestants. Its flowing language and prose rhythm has had a profound influence on the literature of the past 400 years. The King James Version present on the Bible Gateway matches the 1987 printing. The KJV is public domain in the United States.

This book is a work of fiction. Names, characters, places, and incidents are either products of the author's imagination or used fictitiously. Any similarity to actual people, organizations, and/ or events is purely coincidental.

Cover photo credit: Aries 70 Studio, DepositPhotos

Cover design by Tandem Services

To my sibs—Amy, Rick, and Rusty.
I loved growing up with you, but I love you more now.

*Wait for the Lord. Be strong and let your heart take courage.
Yes, wait for the Lord.*

Psalm 27:14

ONE

Summer Time Blues

Saturday afternoon, August 3, 1968

"Here you go, Mom. Let me help you." Thea put the cup to her mother's lips.

"Thea?"

Phil. Her hand jiggled, sloshing the red drink down the front of her mom's new dress. "Oh!" She needed to take care of her mother, but more than that she wanted to run. Anywhere. She grabbed a wedding-embossed napkin and started dabbing. "I'm so sorry, Mom. Phil, you made me jump."

And he stood there in his suit and tie, hair parted so that little curl turned up on his forehead. "I can see that. I'm sorry, Mrs. Salem, for startling Thea."

Mom smiled up at him, appearing not in the least upset. *My side, Mother!*

"I'll get more. Phil, would you stay with her while I do?" She'd never wanted to speak to him again. Now she requested a favor. It galled her.

"Of course."

Of course, she mimicked in her brain. So easy for him to say. She turned in the direction of the punch bowl. One of them might have said something besides responding so agreeably. *Don't go there.* She sucked in a breath, refilled the cup and returned. "Here you are. Not one word, Phil, until she has a sip." That tickled her mom, and she sputtered on herself. More dabbing with the napkin.

Phil was obedient, at least and remained silent until Mom had her punch. He even accepted the cup from her to put it on the table behind him while Thea wiped Mom's mouth with another napkin. "It's great to see you both. I'm glad you were able to attend, Mrs. Salem."

"Oh, she doesn't let much hold her back. As long as she has her wheels, we can get around pretty good, huh, Mom?"

Mom nodded. She didn't enjoy speaking in public since the stroke. People often didn't understand her. But her smile remained bright, and she was flashing it at Phil. *Knock it off, Mother.*

"What have you been up to, Thea?"

Should she say there'd been no one else? Did he even care? "Mom and I have our routines. We keep busy." So now you know. She heard her mother's training in her head—*We don't behave that way*—and the longer the pause, the worse it got. She blinked and forced her smile to grow. "And what about you, Phil? How is Penn State?"

He straightened his glasses. "Still there. I teach four classes and one outdoor lab where I take students to different battle-fields. The rest of my schedule allows me to work on my disser-tation. I should get to my boards by the end of school. Might be in time for graduation."

"I'm happy for you." *Liar, liar.* Why'd he have to look so doggone cute with that chin dimple and wayward curl? "It was nice talking with you, but I'd better take Mom home so—" Mom grabbed her hand, pulling her close.

Thea tucked her hair behind her ear and leaned so Mom could whisper. "Oo ga tak wid him. Meye geme hum."

She shook her head. What was her mom thinking? Go talk

with him? Even if Aunt Mel could get her home, she'd not spend time alone with Phil Carpenter ever again. No way. "That's okay, Mom. No problem."

Then there was a problem.

Aunt Mel walked over, and Mom motioned for her to listen. The whole while, Thea felt the heat building in her face. What must Phil be thinking? Did she care what he thought?

"I can take your mom home, sweetie. A grand idea so you can talk with your young man. Val says it's been a while since you've seen him."

"He's not my—"

Mom patted her hand. Thank you very much.

Aunt Mel blew her a kiss and wheeled her mother, The Betrayer, toward the exit.

Thea turned back to Phil. He had a funny smirk on his face. As if he found that hilarious. Just one chuckle, buster, and *bam, zoom!*

"Would you like to dance, or would you rather sit and chat?" He waited for her answer as if he'd offered her something worth choosing.

She didn't want to be near him. It was too painful. But if she said or did what she wanted, she'd embarrass the bride, who was her best friend. "Let's sit." At least then she wouldn't have to feel his arms around her.

He led her to a table in the corner of the room. "Would you like some punch?"

She shook her head, thoughts of spilling it on her own dress flashing through her mind.

He sat, resting his elbow on the table, his cheek on his fist. "I thought you'd be a bridesmaid, if not the maid of honor."

"Maid of honor was Connie's sister. That was a given. She asked me to be a bridesmaid, but I needed to stay with Mom."

He glanced at the table. "Oh."

"But I made the bridesmaids dresses." Why was it important he knew that?

He caught her gaze. "You did? I should have known. You did a fine job, Thea."

She hated how his approval melted her resolve the tiniest bit. If she wasn't careful, she'd be headed for more heartache. And she couldn't afford that again. "So, when did you return for the wedding?"

He pulled his glasses off and polished the lenses with an edge of the tablecloth. *You don't fool me, mister.*

"You were already in town?" Why did that bother her?

He cleared his throat, checked for missed specks on his wire-frames and returned them to his face. "I've been here for the summer. Figured you didn't want to see me."

"You were probably right." She added the probably to be nice for her mother's sake. And Connie's. "Guess you figured this would be neutral territory, and you'd be safe, is that it?"

He got that funny smirk again. "That's it. Your brother mentioned you hit hard." Great, another traitor in the family. "But I've wanted to know how you're doing."

"All you had to do was call."

"Would you have taken my call?"

Would she? At first, perhaps. But after all this time, nah. "We should change the subject. Tell me about Pennsylvania."

He relaxed. "Well, there's a lot more hills. Not flat like here. And the winter is colder. But to have all those historic places so close, it's amazing." Now he was sharing his passion, and she saw the Phil she used to know. "I take trips to the sites even without my classes. I walk the areas—Valley Forge blows my mind."

"I'm happy for you." And this time she was. He loved reading about all the geographic locales of the American Revolution. Though she wasn't as big a fan, she'd always enjoyed when he got off on one of his tangents. It brought things to life. He understood the people, those minor stories not shared in history classes.

"Are you sure you don't want to dance? You used to love to."

She wanted to say she used to love a lot of things, but he

tugged on her hand, and she acquiesced.

He turned her into his arms as the first notes of "Cherish" by The Association carried her back to other times in his arms.

Was there was any oxygen the room? How could he do this? Didn't it bring back memories for him? She kept space between them, and there was no way she'd rest her head on his shoulder. If she remained stiff, if she refused to melt into his embrace, she stood a fighting chance.

The song ended after an eternity, and he guided her to the table. "Thea, we've known each other too long. You once called me your friend. Could we be friends?"

Friends? All the thoughts and tears and pain screamed at her. Remember what he did! But her heart also remembered things. Things such as how he taught her how to tell a real antique comb-back Windsor chair from a fake. And how he listened and stayed by her when Daddy died. Maybe if she kept the wall partway up, she might handle it. Maybe if she had no expectations other than mere friendship. Maybe if her stupid heart would do its job and not get all crazy the moment he glanced at her over his glasses before he pushed them up his nose. She might have that fighting chance.

"Sure, why not? Friends. We can do that."

He tipped his head, as if trying to decide if she meant it or was just talking.

"Yes, Phil, I'm willing to be friends."

He smiled. The cute smile that made her pulse race. Stupid pulse. Friends aren't supposed to make that happen. Some fighting chance.

THIS WAS A MISTAKE. Phil wished he hadn't let Jerry talk him into coming. He knew he'd run into Thea, and pretending changed nothing. Besides, he hated how things ended between them.

Why'd he push to be friends? Wasn't that the part that hurt? "If we had punch, we could make a toast to friendship." He was trying too hard.

She smiled.

About time. That phony stuff earlier was worse than her anger.

"Okay, you may get me a cup."

He stood. The tablecloth and centerpiece moved with him. He caught the bowl of floating flowers but drenched his shirt cuff. The cloth had hooked to his belt buckle. His face heated a million degrees while he untangled himself. A quick glance, and he spotted Thea working to keep her laugh at bay. "Go ahead. I'm still a klutz."

She shook her head but grinned. "I was thinking it was something I would do."

That was kind. He tried standing again and found the punchbowl, returning with cups for both of them.

"Thank you." She held hers aloft and waited for him to clink with her.

"To us as friends, you and me, through thick and thin, may we always be." He touched her glass with his.

"You still have a way with words." She took a sip and set the cup back on the table.

"Words are important, Thea. They make us laugh and cry, they can vindicate us, anger us, protect us, change our minds. Words are powerful."

"You really believe that? What about actions?" Now her hands splayed on the tabletop as if she wanted to push everything away. Had he gone too far?

"Actions are important too. If I must choose between, I prefer actions. But don't dismiss the power words wield. What would our world be if John Adams hadn't lifted his voice in the Continental Congress? Or if Luther hadn't pinned his theses to that door in Germany. How many slogans can you recite? Words pack a wallop."

She raised her hands. "I surrender. Words are powerful. But I still say actions carry more weight."

"We can agree on that." He cleared his throat. "So, what are you reading these days?"

"Can't get away from words, huh?" She winked at him. "I'm reading an Agatha Christie. *By the Pricking of My Thumbs*. You?"

"I picked up David McCullough's *The Johnstown Flood*. It boggles my mind how that happened. I wish he'd write about John Adams. He's the one to tell that story."

"No, you are. You have the knowledge and passion. You should do it."

"Change my dissertation into a novel? I don't have that talent. But I hope I do a faithful job with what I turn in to the board." She gazed at him with an openness he'd missed for so long. For a year. Could he keep his heart under control and not let her twist it to bits again? Well, he *was* the one who brought up the friend word. He only had himself to blame.

"What other safe topics shall we cover?" She glanced away as she spoke. It was still hard for her too.

He was foolish to think they'd merely talk because of this neutral setting. It was a wedding for goodness sake. It might have been theirs. "Who was that dancing with your brother?"

"Oh, that's Hien Wheaten. She was married to Mike Wheaten before he was killed in Vietnam. Aunt Melanie brought her back with her. Beau fell for her like a ton of bricks. They've just started dating, but you can bet it's serious."

"She seems nice."

"Oh, she is. I'll enjoy having her for a sister-in-law."

"Aren't you rushing that a bit? You said they'd only started."

She waved her hand. "Not really. They're the only ones who don't know how this ends, and I kinda think they do. When you see them together, you'll understand."

He searched for another safe topic. "Where are Connie and Jerry going for their honeymoon?"

"They're heading to French Lick. It's only for a few days. I'm surprised Jerry is leaving the paper as long as he is. But I expect his mom will put out a bare-bones edition to keep it running until he's back."

He nodded. French Lick, Indiana was a popular honeymoon destination. "Thea, I don't leave for another week. Do you think we might go out?" What was he saying? His mouth was spouting things without checking with his brain. *Say no, say no.*

She paused, her thumbnail to her teeth. "I don't know."

"We could meet for a Coke at the café. That should be simple enough." Why didn't he let this go?

"I guess. Or, would you prefer to come to dinner tomorrow after church? Do you still go to church? I saw your dad but not you this summer."

She caught him again. "I was afraid we'd run into each other, so I've attended a little place in Peru."

"Oh, yeah. Well, since you don't have to duck me now, you can come back."

He chuckled. "Guess that's right. Should I bring my dad to lunch? Otherwise he's by himself."

"Yes, bring him. Mom will like it. Hien and Aunt Mel are coming too." She glanced around. "Did your dad attend the wedding? I didn't see him."

He shook his head, remembering his father waving from the porch. "No, he wasn't up to it. But he won't miss church tomorrow, so we'll be there."

"And you can meet Hien." She gazed at him a moment and then drummed her fingers on the table. "Maybe I should be getting home."

"How are you going to do that?"

A funny expression crossed her face. "Aunt Mel took Mom home in the Tank. And she rode here with Hien in the Mustang. That means Beau's going back with Hien, and I don't have a ride." She hopped up. "Oh! And Aunt Mel can't get Mom in the house by herself. I need to leave."

"No problem, I can drive you."

She didn't wait for him but headed past the tables.

Stupid, stupid, stupid. Just like before. Was it possible to be only friends? Could his heart take it again if it wasn't? Well, he wouldn't strand her at the reception. He followed her to his car.

She stood by the door waiting for him to unlock it.

Which he did. Even held it for her too.

She climbed in.

But it was more than that. It was like she'd crawled inside herself. Withdrawn, just when they'd found a patch of common ground. Suddenly they were back to a year ago, her so worried and closing him out. His only choice was to take her home.

He pulled in the drive.

The ladies sat beneath the old sycamore tree, one on a bench, the other in her wheelchair. They laughed about something.

Thea barely let him stop before she hopped from the car, racing toward them. "I realized you wouldn't be able to get Mom in the house. I'm so sorry, Aunt Melanie."

"Oh, honey, we knew you or Beau would be along. We found some shade, and I brought out glasses of lemonade. We're having a grand ol' time."

Phil noticed Thea didn't relax, but as least she stopped panicking. "I probably ought to go, unless you need me?"

Thea flashed him the grin that ripped his heart from his chest. "Yes! Please! Phil, can you help Mom back into the house? It's easier with a man to get her up the steps."

Funny how Mrs. Salem's smile drooped at Thea's words. Still, she didn't stop the plan.

"Sure. Tell me what to do."

He and Thea worked as a team and got her mom on the porch.

"We'll take it from here, Phil. Thanks."

And with that, Thea dismissed him. Again.

She really didn't understand the power of her words.

TWO

Lady Willpower

Sunday, August 4, 1968

THEA'S STOMACH CHURNED THROUGHOUT CHURCH. PASTOR Bob probably had preached a great sermon, but all she could think of was how to retract her dinner invitation. Why'd she invite Phil in the first place?

She knew why. It was insurance that she wouldn't be alone with him. It seemed like a smart idea, but now she'd chewed her thumbnail to the quick. There was a pot roast in the oven, and Beau brought the dining table in from storage when she let slip that she'd invited Phil and his dad for Sunday dinner. Once Mom came home after her stroke, the dining room became her bedroom. But for special occasions, they'd bring in the table and chairs, push furniture around the living room, and make it work. Beau did all that. For her. Because of her foolish slip.

And she noticed that look in his eye while he set it up, even though he said nothing. Her brother hoped she and Phil would get back together. He had that same stupid gaze now while holding Hien's hand. The family had gathered outside after the service. What was left of her thumbnail found her teeth again.

"Hey Phil, over here." Beau was way too excited.

Phil wandered over with his father. She'd always liked Mr. Carpenter. This—whatever it was between her and his son—had nothing to do with him. She should have kept in better contact. "It's good to see you all." The men shook hands with her brother and Beau introduced Hien and Phil.

"Thea's got a pot roast going. Should be ready when we get there. You want to follow us home?" You'd think Beau was hungry or something.

Mr. Carpenter glanced at Phil, who pulled off his glasses and started polishing them. He hadn't mentioned it to his father. "Uh, Dad, I meant to tell you. We've been invited to the Salems' for lunch."

Thea glanced at her mom who watched the entire exchange. Did she hope they would come? Or back out?

"Why that sounds like a grand idea. Phil, you should have said something before. We'd have brought dessert."

Phil slid his glasses in place. "Sorry, Dad. Sure, we can follow you."

Forty-five minutes later they were all at the house, and everyone but Thea sat at the table. Mom was so excited that on the way home, she tried talking about it, saying she hoped they'd get back together.

Whatever possessed Thea to agree to that stupid friend idea?

Thea burned herself twice getting the roast onto the serving plate. The gravy was on the salty side. The mashed potatoes were too thin. It was a disaster. The sooner she served this mess and sent that man out of her house, the better she'd feel.

"Anything I can do to help?" Hien spoke behind her, jarring her thoughts.

"Oh, I didn't hear you come in." Thea wiped her hands on her apron. "Yes, please. Help me load the food on the cart? Nothing came out right. I hope nobody gets sick."

"Now you are talking silly. No one will get sick. I am sure it is better than you give it credit." Hien gave her a squeeze.

"Thanks, I needed that. Here, you take the potatoes and gravy boat. I'll add the rest." She would enjoy having Hien for a sister-in-law.

Hien smiled and added the dishes to the serving cart.

Thea brought the meat and a bowl of roasted vegetables. Once the cart was loaded, she pushed it to the table and began passing the food before claiming her chair. Across from Phil. Man, she wished she'd caught that in time to rectify it.

Family and guests all sent murmurs of approval back to her, but she only noticed the flaws.

Beau tried to keep the conversation going. She could've kissed him for that. Phil asked a few questions, trying to draw her in, and she really did her best to answer. But her mind was in such turmoil, self-doubt attacking on one side, while fear of getting hurt again charged from the other. No telling which emotion was stronger, but this much she figured out—it all surfaced when Phil Carpenter resurfaced in her life.

There was only one solution. She couldn't be alone with him again. No matter what. If it was this painful in a crowd, alone would be lethal to her sanity.

Thea excused herself to get the dessert—strawberries over angel food cake with whipped cream. Simple, cool and refreshing. She'd baked the cake yesterday, sliced the strawberries last night, and over-whipped the cream just now. Her hands shook plating each dessert.

Back at her chair, she tried cutting off bites of cake and pushing them around on her plate. Her stomach flipped too much to eat. She hoped no one noticed. But a glance in her mother's direction spoiled that thought. Mom had that goofy half grin beaming her way. Thea sighed.

Hien covered her hand. "Do not worry about the kitchen. Mil will help you put Aunt Val to bed, and Beau will assist me with the dishes."

"I will?" Beau winked at the girl who had him twisted in

happy little knots. "Oh, right, I will." He smiled like he'd won the Indy 500.

"Now you'll have time. Sit on the swing. Go for a walk." Hien patted her hand.

Thea glanced at the faces around the table. Each of the women—Hien, Aunt Mel, Mom—they all beamed at her like some conspiracy. Beau and Mr. Carpenter chuckled. But Phil, poor Phil, he polished his glasses for all he was worth. He didn't want to be alone with her any more than she wanted to be alone with him. At least that was something.

"Thank you." Arguing would cause a scene. Too many loved ones wanted to help her. Unfortunately, it wasn't what she required.

While helping Mom get changed and into her bed, she tried speaking low to Aunt Mel. "I'm not sure but I think I'm coming down with a bug. My stomach is unsettled. Maybe I should go lie down for a bit after we get Mom comfortable."

Of course, Aunt Mel checked her forehead for a nonexistent fever. "You're just nervous. Your mom says he used to be your steady. It's natural to have butterflies after a time. But I'll bet if you talk, it will become easier." She cupped Thea's cheek and patted it.

And then Mom caught her hand and pulled her close. "Guh, taw wi hum. E tum."

Thea wanted to cry. Just talking with him yesterday about safe topics nearly broke her in two. It wasn't time. It would never be time. *I can't go talk with him, Mom. Please don't make me.*

But once Mom was in bed, Aunt Mel practically pushed her to the porch. Mr. Carpenter sat in the swing. Phil paced in front of the railing. If she joined his father, perhaps the older man would stay with them. She plopped next to him.

"That was a mighty fine meal, Thea. You are some cook."

"Thank you, Mr. Carpenter. All I saw were my mistakes. But you are kind."

"Are you kidding? I haven't eaten that well since I can't remember when. Been a month of Sundays. That's for sure. I'll tell you one thing, though. If that wasn't up to snuff, I don't know what is." Phil's dad could make her feel better any time.

She flashed him a grin. "So, who usually cooks for you?"

"Margie or another at the Breadville Café. I doubt it's your brother doing the cooking there." He slapped his knee and guffawed.

Beau was technically the owner of the café. He invested to help keep it open and made sure the people there knew how to cook. Especially since he couldn't do it to save his life—unless it was on the barbecue grill.

Phil pushed his glasses up on his nose. "Thanks again, Thea, for having us over. We probably ought to start for home."

"Are you sure?" Why'd she ask that?

"Yeah, we don't want to wear out your hospitality."

She smoothed out the skirt of her apron she'd forgotten to remove. "I'll grab some of that roast for you. We've plenty of leftovers." A timely excuse to step out of Phil's presence.

"There's no need—"

"Son, let her get the meat."

Thea laughed at that. She really liked Mr. Carpenter.

Moments later, she returned with a covered dish and handed it to Phil's dad before she kissed him on the cheek. "I'll cook for you anytime, Mr. Carpenter."

His eyes grew rounder and he looked a bit surprised and then a little pleased and a whole lot tickled as he let slip a giggle. "I might take you up on that, young lady." He patted her shoulder before heading for the steps. "C'mon son, let's take this food home. I think a roast beef sandwich is calling my name."

Phil smiled his trademark smirk and followed his dad. As they reached their car, Thea overheard what she wished she hadn't. "Son, you never should've let that girl get away."

PHIL DROVE FASTER than he intended, but the sooner he got home, the sooner he could put distance between him and his father. Not that he didn't love his old man—he hardly remembered his mother who died before he started first grade. His father ruled his world for a very long time. But the entire ride to the farm was one giant game of Clue. Dad was on a mission to learn what happened. Why'd they break up? Or to quote his father, why'd he let her get away?

If his dad only knew.

"Son, a girl like Thea doesn't grow on trees. You won't find another like her. Can't you work things out? You two belong together."

"She wraps up some roast beef for you and kisses you on the cheek, and now she's Miss Universe, Julia Child, and an angel all rolled into one, huh? It's not that easy, Dad." He shook his head.

"Then tell me what happened."

Phil pulled to a stop by their back door, put the car in park and cut the engine. "She said no, Dad. That's what happened. She said no." He watched to see if his father figured it out, that it hurt to be around her. Still. After a year. It plain hurt.

"So, you gave up?"

"Gave up? Dad, I asked her to marry me and she said no. Not let's give it a little more time or let me think. Just no. It was over." He climbed from the Chevy Impala, pocketed his keys, and leaned against the vinyl roof. "They'd hired me at Penn State, and I had to leave. I was willing to try the long-distance thing. She wasn't. But I thought perhaps, after this past year, we might be friends. So, I talked with her at the wedding yesterday. It was an enormous mistake, and I'm still raw." He shrugged. "There's nothing to give up. It's all gone." He pushed away and walked around the car to the house.

His father remained next to the passenger door, not moving. "What do you plan to do?"

"Right now? I'm going in to take a Sunday afternoon nap."

Truth was that sleep eluded him most of the night. He could use a snooze. Every time he closed his eyes, Thea's smiling face materialized, drawing him in and then, *bam*. She withdrew into that other person. How did she morph like that? He didn't understand where she'd gone.

In fact, that was something else. Before, she was so active in the choir at church, singing the occasional special with her Dusty Springfield alto that enveloped him like caramel. But she wasn't even up front today. He almost asked her, but changed his mind. Too many folks there. And she didn't seem to want to be alone with him, anyway. One more mystery someone else could unravel.

Instead of waiting for Dad, he went straight to his room and flopped on the bed. Stretched out, he gave in to his craving. His fingers felt for the knob, pulling open the drawer of his nightstand which hid what used to be displayed. With his heart pounding in his ears, he felt around until his fingers latched onto the cool metal. This used to sit next to his lamp. It received his first greeting each morning and was the last thing he glimpsed before falling asleep. Her college yearbook picture signed *Love always, Thea*.

A part of him wanted to throw the blamed thing across the room shouting *Liar*. The other part, the civilized part, was sure he'd regret that act, so he returned it, his fingertips brushing against something soft. A velvet box. He took it out and opened it. The diamond ring cost him every cent he'd saved. He wanted the best for her. With a snap he closed it. He should sell it. But he couldn't bring himself to do that. He dropped it inside and shoved the drawer closed. Where had he picked up such masochistic tendencies?

He rolled to his side, his back to the Thea drawer, and willed himself to sleep.

An hour later, he threw his pillow against the far wall and gave up. He did not understand if Thea tortured him or if he tortured himself with her. But it involved torture, and she was there. Every time he closed his eyes.

Work. That's what he needed. His briefcase lay open at his old desk in the corner. He wasn't ready to type, but he could write things in longhand. There was enough to begin, so he scanned through his index cards, arranging them in order, and began forming sentences about John Adams. He was the most underrated president the country ever produced. A brilliant mind, a passion for standing for what's right, and a wife who was also his best friend. Phil nearly snorted. They were in love and yet were the best of friends, depending on each other, sharing their deepest thoughts with one another. Though the revolution separated them for years at a time, still they trusted their love. He thought that's what he and Thea had.

But he was wrong.

Great, even with his work, Thea manifested herself somehow. No, he would focus.

He tried writing again, scratched through it, made another attempt and ripped the sheet from his legal pad. Crumpled into a tight ball, he tossed it at the trashcan. "Two points."

He tore off a second paper and crumpled it, lofting it into the receptacle. "And he scores again." He cheered his efforts.

He was standing on his desk chair, ripping the third page free when his dad opened the door. "You okay, son?"

Phil jumped to the floor and pulled off his glasses, tossing them on the desk. He ran his fingers through his hair while he chuckled without mirth. "No, Dad, I'm not. I'm a wreck. I can't think, I can't sleep. I've got to finish my dissertation, or I won't be ready for my boards. My adviser must approve it just to get me on the schedule, and right now there's nothing to approve. I've been cataloging data, I have copious notes, and not a brain cell left in my head that will stick to the topic. The most successful thing I've accomplished is shooting free throws in the trash."

He glanced at his dad's cheesy grin. "You still love her."

"Tell me something I don't know."

Dad sat on the bed. "Okay, I will. Back when I first met your mother, I knew right away she was the one for me. But she had no clue I existed. She was dating this other fella. He was more popular, athletic. Almost as good looking as me. Oh, and he was a townie. A rich kid. Well, I didn't stand a chance. But I couldn't get her out of my mind. We had a few classes together, and I had to see her, too often with that fella."

"What did you do, Dad?"

"I made myself indispensable. That's what I did. I studied up on anything I thought she might need and helped her with homework. Gave her a reason to see me. And once she did, the old Carpenter charm got her."

Phil chuckled again. It wasn't the first time he'd heard the story, but he enjoyed how Dad told it. "I wish it were that easy. I'm not fighting against some other guy. Something has gotten ahold of her. It has to do with her mother. Whenever Mrs. Salem comes into the discussion, she's another person. I don't even know her."

"Maybe she's afraid. Not that long after she lost her father, Val had the stroke. She might fear losing her too."

Phil rubbed his face and put on his glasses. "Yeah, I'm sure you're right. But her fear is big enough that she's willing to throw out what we had. She's gotta work through it, Dad. There's nothing I can do." He picked up his legal pad and waved it. "And I gotta get this written or I'll never get my adviser's approval or have my defense scheduled with the board. I'd better go back to Pennsylvania."

His dad stood. "So soon? Don't you have another week?"

"I do, but I can't handle another day, let alone seven more days. I'll lose my mind."

Dad squeezed his shoulder. "At least don't start back tonight. The drive's too long. You won't get there until two in the morning. It's not safe."

He patted Dad's hand. Another night here would be hard.

But it was only one. Besides, if he ran some wind sprints before bed, he might drop and not even dream. "Sure, I'll wait for morning. We can have breakfast together at the café."

THREE

Yummy, Yummy, Yummy

Wednesday morning, October 16, 1968

THEA PUSHED HER SHOPPING CART THROUGH THE BAKING aisle and heard her name. Turning, she spotted Phil's dad waving. "How are you, Mr. Carpenter?"

"Fair to middlin', I reckon. You?"

"Doing well, thank you. Just taking advantage of the Wednesday sales and coupons to stock up on supplies and get my green stamps." She gave him a wink. "Don't suppose I should bake you a batch of cookies?"

He laughed. "That's what I like about you, Thea. I never have to hint around. Sure. I'd love some. Think I might get a few oatmeal chocolate chip? Once you try those, it's plain wrong to use raisins."

She smiled. "You've got it. I'll make them for you special. How about I bring them on Sunday?"

His grin was like Phil's.

She winced from the stabbing pain in her chest.

"Deal, missy. And while I'm at it, I can't eat a huge batch and keep this youthful figure. Plus, it's hard on you to fix just a

31

few. Maybe you oughta send some over to Pennsylvania. There's a college professor who might appreciate a cookie or two."

"Mr. Carpenter, are you trying to start something?"

She'd seen Phil try that innocent look too. Those Carpenter men.

"Me? Start something? Nah, just being helpful. I'll let you get back to your shopping young lady, and see you on Sunday." He turned his cart the other direction. Before rounding the corner, he glanced over his shoulder and waved.

She waved, too, but dropped her smile once he was out of sight. That man! He was as bad as his son. Worse! At least Phil had left her alone for the last two months. Two whole months. Why did that depress her?

Her list held only a few more items. She hustled to grab them and get through the check-out line for home. Even there she wore a happy face mask. But in the Tank, she could be herself. She started the engine of the big ol' Lincoln Continental and rolled down her window to enjoy the Indian Summer weather. Beau had the station set to WLS in Chicago. The commercial ended as she turned from the IGA parking lot followed by David Ruffin's distinctive voice pouring out her heart as the Temptations sang "I Wish It Would Rain." She pulled to the curb until she stopped crying.

"Thea?" A tapping on her window frame startled her. Connie. Her friend stared at her. "What's wrong?"

Where had she come from? Thea glanced in the rearview mirror. There was Jerry's Camaro parked behind her. "You want the *Reader's Digest* version? The Temptations made me cry."

Connie continued to stare.

"All right. I ran into Phil's dad at the grocery. He suggested I send cookies to Phil."

"So?"

"So, the younger Mr. Carpenter hasn't spoken to me since the day after your wedding. No letter, no nothing. He makes a point of saying he wants to be friends and gives me the silent treatment for two stinking months. And his dad tells me to bake cookies for him?" There was that anger. She needed it to grow. It would chase all that dopey depression out.

"How dare he? I mean, he shows up, gets me all flustered, and then walks away. I was over him and look what he's done. I think I hate him. Yes! I do! I hate him, and his glasses that keep slipping on his nose, and that curl that likes to droop on his forehead, and how he seems to be so low key and mellow until you get him talking about his passions. I want to hit him. Now! Bake him cookies? I'll bake him cookies all right. I'll make him Ex-Lax cookies and see how he likes them apples."

"Are you done?"

"What?"

"Are you done ranting like a crazy woman? I need to know when I can talk some sense into you." The expression on Connie's face told her she'd gone a little overboard. Or a lot overboard. Yeah, they needed to talk.

Thea took a breath. "Done. What now?"

"I'll follow you, and we'll discuss this like the two amazing and wise and creative women we are."

"How long can you stay? This might take a while."

"I'm here for you, sweetie. I'll call Jerry from your house and let him know where I am. See you at the farm."

She waited until Connie was in her car and then pulled from the curb and headed home. A talk with her friend would do her good.

At the farm, she parked and popped the trunk. Connie helped carry in the paper bags. Once inside, she called Jerry while Thea put the groceries away and pulled out two cans of Sprite with glasses of ice. Not that she was eavesdropping, but with the phone in the kitchen it was hard not to hear all the lovey-dovey stuff. Had she and Phil sounded like that? She hoped not.

She slipped out to check on Mom. Who was napping.

Which was good. Mom hadn't enjoyed a proper night's sleep for a week. She returned to the kitchen as Connie hung up.

"Jerry says hi and to bake him some cookies too. But before we get started, we need to talk." She pulled out a chair and filled her glass. "You still have feelings for the guy, don't you?"

Thea's face heated, thinking of the rant she'd let loose in the car. "Um, I guess I do."

"So, make the first move."

"What? That's a Sally Ann Meister strategy. It's not what I do."

"Oh, honey, there's a lot of wiggle-room in there. You can be the nice girl and make the first move. It's not too forward. Trust me on this. How do you think I got Jerry?"

"What do you mean?"

She giggled. "You remember how I'd be over here with you and he'd be here to see Beau? And he'd always say he should marry you because you are the best cook in the county?"

Thea nodded. "I thought you always hated that. I cringed when he said that around you because you were so interested in him and he was clueless."

"Well, I could get upset or pay attention. He loves to eat? I can make pies. I found excuses for my pies to tempt him until he took notice of me. I also learned as much as possible about him so I could talk about his favorite subjects."

"What about him talking about your favorite subjects?"

"That's one of the enjoyable things about my husband. Once he took notice, he got curious about me and took an interest in what I liked. If he hadn't, I would have gotten bored. See? I wasn't trying to do anything phony. Only spark an interest. If the spark became a flame, great. But if I waited for him to notice me without starting something, I wouldn't be wearing these rings." She flashed her fingers.

"I already know Phil's interests. And I used to listen while he told me about them." She pictured him now, getting excited about the latest thing he'd uncovered concerning the founding fathers.

"And he usually had one of your cookies in his mouth when he did, right?" Connie peered her in the eyes, daring her to deny it.

"Okay, so he liked my cookies. But remember how Sally Ann worked her campaign to get Beau? This still sounds a lot like something she'd pull, not me."

Sally Ann Meister had all but roped and tied her brother. He still got a little deer-in-the-headlights when she approached at church.

"You are not the forward type, and this isn't the same as Sally Ann's campaign. Remember, Beau was never in love with her. Phil, at least, was in love with you at one time. You're merely fanning the embers."

Was Connie even listening? "But he's the one who found me at your reception. He's the one who said he wanted to be friends and then took off two days later without saying goodbye or writing or anything. Not exactly friendly, if you ask me."

"I'm guessing he either scared himself or you were too stand-offish, and he gave up."

"Me? I did nothing…other than avoid him."

"When was that?" Connie rested her chin on her fist, reminding her of Phil doing that at the reception. Everything reminded her of him. She could scream.

"At Sunday dinner. He'd asked me out, and I thought it better to be here in case Mom needed me, so I invited him to join us after church. He wondered if he should bring his dad, but then he didn't even tell him. Mr. Carpenter learned about it when Beau started talking with them after the service."

"Awful convenient."

"I know. That's what I don't get. He wants to be friends. Then he doesn't want to come."

"I mean you. Awful convenient to have your family surrounding you, to keep you from getting too close to him."

"That's not fair."

"No, not fair is my best friend erecting walls all over the place, not letting anyone get close. You've done it with me, and you did it to him. It's been like that since your mom's stroke."

Thea glanced away. That couldn't be true. But the sting of her words said different. "What can I say? I gotta make sure Mom is safe. Neither of us will survive if she has another."

Connie reached over and covered her hand. "Honey, you are not alone. I'm here for you. And I will help you. Now let's get baking so I can get those cookies in the mail for you today."

Saturday morning, October 19, 1968

The noise at his door caught Phil off guard. He'd hit his stride on his opening paragraph when the insistent knock pulled his mind to the present. "Coming."

His mailman stood on the other side, holding out a package. "Here you go. It won't fit in your mailbox."

"Thanks." Phil opened the screen and accepted it. No return address, but the postmark read Breadville. He didn't need to search for the sender's name. The handwriting revealed her identity. The same handwriting graced that photo in his nightstand at the farm. Thea.

He closed the door with his foot and stared. What'd she send? Why'd she send anything? "Ugh!" He tossed the box on the counter of his kitchenette.

He'd made progress. It took leaving home and driving for eight hours and then sleeping another ten before he'd pushed her from his thoughts enough to work on his dissertation. He'd written and submitted his outline and been approved. Now he just needed to write the blasted paper. And here she was again. He had nowhere else to run.

He stared at the box, willing it to explain itself. Should he open it? He had no other way to discover what she'd sent. Did he want to know? Could he stare and not succumb to curiosity? However, once he knew, he could never un-know. The mystery would be answered. What if he threw it away and pretended he never got it? Not that he foresaw being asked, "What'd Thea send?" Could be all Breadville was aware she mailed him a box. In a small town, everyone's business was big news. So, should he open? Or stare? Or toss? Open, stare, toss, open, stare, toss…

He'd drive himself insane.

Taking a paring knife from the drawer, he sliced through the tape. An envelope lay on top of another box. Another box? She was a master of torture, that one. His fingers trembled but still reached inside. He opened the envelope and withdrew a brief letter.

Dear Phil,

    I ran into your dad at the grocery, and he suggested you might enjoy some cookies. I think oatmeal chocolate chip were your favorite, right? If not, tell me. I'll send the right ones next time.

    Your friend,

    Thea

She baked him cookies? She baked him oatmeal chocolate chip cookies?

He tore the lid off the inside box and there, nestled between sheets of wax paper, lay layer after layer of his all-time favorite. He sniffed. Oatmeal and brown sugar with walnuts and chocolate chips. Not only that. Thea crafted the most amazing cookies on the planet. He loved being in the kitchen when she made them. The universe smelled like happiness. He snatched one and bit it in half. Oh, it was better than he remembered. So good his knees grew weak as the chocolate morsels melted over his tongue. He grabbed two more and fell into his chair. This was the best. She sent him cookies.

She. Sent. Him. Cookies.

Danger, Will Robinson. What did she want? What was her motive? Was there a cost to this?

Memories flooded. The two of them sitting in her kitchen, munching on a fresh out-of-the-oven cookie, almost too hot to touch, while telling her what he'd learned about John Adams's trip to Russia as an ambassador. How sick the man got. She listened to every word. Asking questions. Making him think. Or go research. Maybe she wanted to support his work? Maybe she had no ulterior motive. Maybe the good Thea sent the cookies when Stranger Thea wasn't looking.

No matter. They didn't live in the same state. He and the cookies were together, and he'd enjoy them. No law insisted he must see Thea, or Other Thea, and get his heart stomped.

He hopped up, poured himself a glass of milk and grabbed three more cookies. Time to work on his paper. He sat back at his desk, his pen poised over the page. While a cookie dangled from his lips, he waited for the inspiration. But he'd lost his train of thought. It flew out the window with that knock. Now he had zilch.

He'd had it, ready to write when the knock came. What happened?

Thea happened. She did it again. This was not fair.

He got up and paced the one-room apartment. On purpose he'd kept all traces of her from this place. No photos, no old letters, no souvenirs. Any gift she'd given stayed back at his dad's. He did not let her poison this place with memories he had no power to hold at bay. Now she'd slipped past his barriers. His boundaries. Her cookie aroma would always be in his mind, associated with this apartment.

He should curse her. Yet he really couldn't. She hadn't done a vicious thing to him. She'd sent a friendly gesture. And he was the who started this friends fiasco. Okay. If that's how it was, fine.

He pulled out a sheet of stationery.

Dear Thea,

You remembered! You care! You want me back!

He crumpled it. *Idiot.*

Again.

Dear Thea,

Thank you for the cookie surprise. Yes, you remembered. Those are my favorites. What a ~~kind thoughtful~~ friendly gesture.

They accepted my outline for my dissertation, so now I am working on the paper. With approval for that, I can get busy on my chapters. I have so much information on my note cards, I'm not sure I can use it all. But I keep going, step by step, and one day I'll chew the last bite of this elephant.

My classes are going well. I find I enjoy teaching more than I thought I would. At first it was a means to getting my doctorate and doing research, but teaching has its rewards. I like the interaction with the students, and when I read the papers of those who are passionate about history, it's like finding hope.

Please thank my dad for me. I'm glad he had the idea. I also appreciate the time you took to bake and send. Your cookies are as wonderful as I remember. Thank you for thinking of me.

Your friend,

Phil

He read it to himself. It was honest and not pushy. He hoped she would accept it in the spirit of friendship. Of course, he needed to rewrite to fix those strikeouts, but he'd live with that response.

Ten minutes later it was neatly written, folded, and inserted into a stamped, addressed envelope. He grabbed his sweater and walked to the post office before he changed his mind.

It wasn't far. A quarter of an hour's worth of walking brought him to the building. As it was Saturday, the place was locked tight. But before he got to the mailbox, a car honked at him.

"Phil? Phil Carpenter?" It was Karen, Dean D'Albany's daughter. She waved from her alpine blue 1969 GTO convertible.

He returned the wave and walked to her car. It was show-room sweet, that's for sure. Must be nice having a daddy who liked to shower those types of gifts.

"What are you doing out here?"

"Gotta mail a letter." He fanned it in the air.

"Do that later. Hop in. I'll take you for a spin in my birthday present."

He shook his head. "I need to do this." He walked away but turned. "If you give me a minute, I'll be right back."

"Sure."

He loped to the box and pulled down the door. Should he? Shouldn't he? He'd taken too long. Now he doubted himself.

"C'mon Phil, let's go."

He dropped the letter in and ran to the car.

FOUR

I'm Gonna Make You Love Me

Thursday afternoon, November 7, 1968

Connie and Hien sat at the kitchen table as Thea read aloud her latest letter from Phil. "You are aware that if there was anything worth reading, I wouldn't be sharing it with you two."

Hien giggled and nodded but Connie got serious, tiny thinking lines forming between her perfect brows. This was a dangerous sign. "He's got his nose too far into his books. Or perhaps our strategies require more proximity to work."

"What do you mean?"

"I mean, you need a vacation. You are overworked and under-appreciated. I'm envisioning a country drive, say to…Pennsylvania."

"Are you crazy?" Thea stared at her friend, who developed a devilish grin.

"Not crazy at all. You gotta be in the same state. Together. He'll hear the message."

"I can't count what all's wrong with your plan. First, how do I get there? I can't commandeer the Tank. That's the only thing we have for transporting Mom in case something happens.

Second, you're talking an eight-hour drive there. I'd have to plan on somewhere to stay before I come back. Most important, who will take care of Mom while I'm gone?"

"Details."

"Essential details!"

"You're just scared. Hien, what do you say?"

Connie may have cornered her, but Thea was curious too.

Hien's glance roved between the women, and she sighed. "I am not used to this. But it is important to face our fears. Let us look at what you said. I can help with parts of it. If I go with you, you would not be alone. We could take my Mustang. Also, Mil very much enjoys helping with Aunt Val. Maybe she would stay the night. Perhaps we could leave early enough and drive back, taking turns so no one gets too tired."

"She's right. You need to face your fears, Thea."

The butterflies dancing *Swan Lake* in her stomach disagreed. "What sort of schedule are you considering?"

Connie perked up. "Well, if you left by six Saturday, you'd arrive by two that afternoon. You can return the next morning. Check on reserving a motel room for Saturday night."

"What if Penn State has a home game? The motels around there fill up fast with football fans."

Connie sighed. "You'll never know until you check. Jerry's got the sports information. I'll call him."

As Connie dialed the number, Thea turned to Hien. "Do you really think Aunt Mel will stay with her while we go?"

"Of course. She loves spending time with your mother."

"And you would be willing to ride along? I feel forward doing this, but it is hard to say no to Connie when she starts steamrolling me. My agreeing to make her bridesmaids dresses was the only reason I got out of her wedding."

Hien chuckled. "She tends to bend people to her will. But she always means well and would never hurt someone on purpose."

"So you see it too." Thea winked, and they shared a smile.

Connie came back. "Jerry says they have a home game. They are playing the University of Miami and are undefeated so it might very well be crowded. Call AAA and ask if they can help get you a room."

Thea sighed, stood and got her AAA card to make the call. Twenty minutes later, she returned with success. "Though I don't understand why we are rushing so fast. Why not wait for another weekend?"

"Because the longer you wait, the better you become at putting it off. So, let's go. You need to get Melanie onboard." Connie paused and stared at Hien a moment, cocking her head to the side and squinting one eye. "I got to ask you something, Hien. Every time you talk about Melanie, you call her Mil. At first, I thought perhaps I didn't hear clearly, but now…Why do you do that?"

Hien laughed. "Beau asked the same question the day we met. Back in Saigon, Pop, I mean Ernest, realized it was difficult for me to know how to address him and Mil. They were Michael's parents, but I had my own. I wanted to be courteous, but it was hard. He suggested I call him Pop. Then he said that the initials for mother-in-law were M-I-L, so I could call Melanie, Mil. She is like my second mother, and although Michael is gone, she is still my Mil."

"That makes sense and sounds like Ernie. He was a great guy. So was Mike. But enough, we've gotta get this girl ready. Hien, please make the arrangements for Melanie to stay with Val. Thea, let's go check your closet."

By six Saturday morning, Hien pulled up by the back door and popped the trunk of her 1965 Ford Mustang. Thea tossed in her overnight bag and an enormous box of oatmeal chocolate chipped goodies. Connie insisted. She felt like an adage experiment. What's the shortest distance to a man's heart? At the moment, she was sure the answer was more direct than a stomach full of cookies. Perhaps she'd seen one too many episodes of *Mod Squad* but a weapon to the chest made more sense. She needed a better attitude.

Connie rolled up then and ran over, enveloping Thea in a huge hug. "You can do this. I know you can. It'll be great!"

Thea hugged back, holding on to the hope her friend was right.

And then they were off. Hien drove the first leg, They stopped every two hours to switch seats, use the facilities and get gas, if necessary. The one not driving navigated using the map Connie dropped off yesterday. She had picked it up from the Kokomo AAA office, and it had their route highlighted, up to Fort Wayne, over into Ohio, past exits for Cleveland and Akron and into Pennsylvania. University Park, the Penn State campus where Phil taught, was in the middle of the state. There was still a ways to go. But crossing into Pennsylvania put the end in sight.

"What will you say to him?" Hien's gaze remained on the road, but Thea was aware of her scrutiny just the same.

"I don't know. I've tried to come up with something clever or funny. I think it'll depend on how he reacts." Her thumbnail was at her teeth again and nearly obliterated.

"What do you mean?"

"Well, if he seems happy to see me, I'll smile and say how I care enough to send the very best, or something lame like that. But if he looks nervous, or scared, or too shocked, I'll probably shove the cookies in his hands and beat it back to the car."

Hien flashed a quick smile. "You will surprise him. That is expected. Shall we go to the motel first?"

"Yes, please. Great idea."

Hien steered according to Thea's instructions, and they checked in at a Howard Johnson's about a mile from the campus.

Thea fiddled with her hair, touched up her lipstick, and backed out.

"You came all this way. You can do it. Besides, do you want

me to face Connie when we return and she learns I let you change your mind?"

Thea laughed. That was good. "How'd you guess the perfect reply?"

"I am learning about you. You would not subject me to that." She chuckled. "And, I think I should give you my keys. You deserve the privacy. I will wait here and pray for you."

Though it terrified her at first, Thea realized Hien was right. Knowing she prayed helped too. She gave the girl a hug. It was time.

She started the car and then turned the engine back off. Her hands trembled. Was she even calm enough to drive? She had to be. Thea restarted and shifted into gear, heading onto the thoroughfare. Five minutes later she pulled in front of Phil's apartment. She wiped her palms on her skirt, gripped the steering wheel, and took a deep breath. The cookie box sat beside her in the passenger seat.

Just when she had enough courage to open her door, his apartment door opened. A blonde in bellbottom jeans and a pink twin set sauntered out, followed by Phil. Her Phil. He locked his door and then followed the blonde to a blue convertible parked a few cars ahead. It must be hers since she went to the driver's side. Phil climbed in the passenger seat. They pulled away.

Thea stood in the street watching as the car shrunk into the horizon. There was nothing left to do. She took the box, set it in front of his door, and drove back to the motel before she fell apart.

"THIS'LL BE A GREAT GAME. Can't wait to see if we stay undefeated." Phil had to admit he kind of enjoyed having Karen pick him up in her car. Though he would have preferred to drive, his old Impala didn't impress like her new goat. It was fun. And he needed fun. He'd had enough pain and heartache. Fun was good.

Plus, Karen had a way of sitting close when they sat together that made his blood pressure elevate. In a good way. She wasn't bad to look at, not at all, with her pale blond hair and green eyes. Though on the short side, she liked to wear those platform heels with the points to appear taller. But it was her personality that gave her height. She appeared larger than life and a tad overwhelming. Again, in a good way. Yeah.

He glanced over at her. She still talked about who would attend the game, who to greet and who carried clout for his boards. She knew everyone. Another perk of having the dean of a major university for a father, not to mention that he chaired the History Department.

Thea would've let him drive and listened to him ramble. But Thea wasn't here. She chose not to be here. Karen opened his eyes to a lot of unfamiliar things. In a good way.

And he liked it. Sort of.

He also noticed the glances from other men when Karen walked with him. Might they be jealous? He'd done nothing to set this all in motion. She called out to him that day last month. But he wasn't about to shove her company away when it provided a lovely distraction. And she had some great ideas for his dissertation. She encouraged him and warned him what to avoid and include. It was definitely a perk having someone aware of all that in his corner.

They found their seats. On the fifty-yard line. Wow. Her dad had some pull, that's for sure.

The game was amazing—a 27-7 win for Coach Paterno's still-undefeated Nittany Lions. Penn State had their bowl game this year. Especially if they maintained this undefeated status for the first time in fifty years.

Afterward, he and Karen grabbed a bite at a small diner that stayed open late only on game nights. A cheeseburger and a chocolate shake sounded perfect about now. Karen claimed she wasn't hungry but preceded to eat his fries. No girl had ever done that before, picking right off his plate. A part of him liked that about her. Karen D'Albany saw what she wanted and went after it. Too bad she was after his fries.

"Phil, you must understand something about me. I don't play around."

He choked on his bite. It took a minute for him to get his breath, and when he did, he stared at her. "That hadn't crossed my mind. Why would you say that?"

"Because I am serious about my goals and choices. I think whoever I build a relationship with needs to understand that and agree."

"What goals do you have?"

She smiled and swiped another fry. "Big ones. Too big for a discussion here tonight. But we need to discuss it if we are to continue seeing each other. Will we continue to see one another?"

He pulled his glasses off and polished the lenses. "Well, I'd considered asking you out for tomorrow afternoon. I thought we might go to Fort Washington and walk around. If that sounds good to you?" He slipped on his glasses.

"I'd like that very much. That'll be an excellent place to talk. You may pick me up at my house at one. Have you met Daddy?"

"Dean D'Albany? In passing, yes. I doubt he remembers me."

She smiled, and for an instant, he thought of the poem about the spider and the fly, but he shook it off. An odd thing to cross his mind.

"It might surprise you. He likes to note all the doctoral candidates. He says it helps to get a feel for them before they present."

So, he was under scrutiny? Great, simply great. "Now that you mentioned that, I probably ought to get home and put in more time on my dissertation. They approved my paper, so now

I build." He smiled and leaned back, hoping he appeared more relaxed than he was.

"Of course."

He waved for the check. The waitress brought it, and he left her a tip that he couldn't afford before heading to the register. Dating got expensive.

Back at the car, he stopped himself from going to the driver's side. This was hers. Tomorrow she could slum it in his. How would she feel about that? Or about dates that didn't cost a lot of money? Would she be satisfied waiting for a guy to get his degree before settling for serious?

Karen pulled up in front of his apartment.

He didn't know her well enough to kiss her, but a peck on the cheek should be okay. Shouldn't it?

"I had a great time. Thanks for the ticket, Karen. I'll be by tomorrow at one." He leaned in to brush a quick kiss, and she turned her head planting one square on the mouth. He drew back.

"I told you I have goals and I don't play around. You think about that. Good night, Phil."

He climbed out but then leaned in. "Good night, Karen,"

She zoomed off as soon as the door closed.

He shook his head. Never in his entire life had he met anyone like Karen D'Albany. To be honest, she scared him some. In a good way. He sort of liked it. Like a roller coaster. But something told him he'd better keep himself buckled.

On the steps, he spotted a box without markings. He unlocked the door and brought it in with him. Where had this come from? Once he had the light on, he noticed his name scrawled across the top, so it was for him. It wasn't packaged as though it came through the mail, no tape or address on it. He lifted the lid and found six dozen of his favorite cookies. Only one person could have sent it. But how did she get it here? Did she know someone who came through town and asked them to drop them off? He should call her. Tomorrow. Tonight he needed to get to his work.

He poured a glass of milk and grabbed a couple cookies before sitting down to his desk. The paper stood ready in the typewriter. He adjusted the roll bar and stretched his fingers. Then, with his hands hovering over the keys, his mind blanked. Again. What was it about her cookies? Did they brainwash him?

He pulled out his earlier pages. Perhaps if he read through them, he could get a running start. Instead he only saw Thea's face floating in his mind's eye.

He still loved her.

This friend thing ripped his insides out. She'd agreed to friendship, and she had followed through, keeping her word. But it was becoming too clear, he wasn't built to be her friend. He needed a full commitment with her, or he needed her gone from his life. This halfway stuff wouldn't cut it. He jumped up from the desk and grabbed the box of cookies, charging out his back door. The alley trash can. He tipped the box and dumped each oatmeal chocolate chip cookie inside, crammed the box after them, and slammed the lid. He remembered that last part in time. Otherwise the raccoons would party.

She would not tempt him with those treats again. He was done. He'd moved on. He was dating Karen now. Even if his heart argued with him.

Thea was his past. He would leave his past in Breadville.

Back in his room, he realized he must tell her in person. It was only right. He owed her that. Christmas break was nearly here. He would inform her at that time.

Then it would be over.

FIVE

Midnight Confessions

Saturday afternoon, November 9, 1968

THEA FUMBLED WITH HER KEY IN THE LOCK UNTIL THE door swung opened.

Hien stood in the doorway. "What happened?"

"We're leaving. Let's go." Thea swiped her hand over her face, grabbed her overnight case, and headed for the door.

Hien snagged her arm. "Thea, talk to me. What happened?"

She dropped her bag and sunk in a heap. "He's with someone else."

"Who?"

"I don't know who. It's doesn't matter. He can have her. I'm going ho-ho-home." The sobs she'd held at bay in the car broke out of their prison and overwhelmed her. She didn't think it possible to hurt this much over him, but she was wrong. It was almost as bad as losing her dad. In some ways worse, because she never doubted her father loved her. Before today, there was a part of her still sure of Phil's love. Despite everything. But now? Oh, now she wouldn't bet a plugged nickel on his love. The pain of that knowledge squeezed the breath from her. She struggled to inhale.

Hien dropped to the floor and wrapped her in an embrace. "It is okay. You are okay." They rocked back and forth while Thea's body shuddered from the wracking sobs.

"I. Just. Wa-a-nt. To. Go. Hooooome."

"That is what we will do. Let me help you to the car and get us checked out of this room."

Thea nodded against Hien's shoulder and sniffed before raising her head. "Th-thank you."

Hien helped her to her feet, handed over her overnight bag, and gathered up her own things. In a matter of minutes, Thea was back at the Mustang in the passenger seat. As soon as Hien returned, they left and only stopped twice for gas, near Youngstown and Lima. Thea felt guilty for not doing her share of driving, just riding with her eyes leaking the entire way, but Hien never said a word about it.

By 11:30 they pulled in at home. Hien got her bag out of the trunk and waited while she walked to the door. Once they crossed the Indiana border, Thea had tried to talk her into staying the night, but Hien reminded her there were still folks in town who liked to gossip. It was one thing to stay there with Aunt Mel when they first arrived. But now that she was dating Beau, there was no reason to feed speculation. Thea understood. She just hated for the girl to go to an empty house on her account.

From the doorway, Thea watched as the Mustang's taillights traveled the driveway to the road and disappeared. She locked the door and tiptoed in.

"What happened?"

Thea jumped. She glanced about in the dim light from the moon peeking through the curtains while her heart pounded in her ears.

Aunt Melanie sat the kitchen table. She was in her bathrobe and clasping her hands about a mug.

"I'm sorry. Did I wake you?" Thea's hand still covered her heart.

"No, sweetie. I was already down here. Wanted some warm milk to help me sleep. Have a lot on my mind. So why are you back?"

Thea pulled out another chair and joined her. "It's a long story."

"I'm not going anywhere, at least not tonight. What happened?"

She sighed. At this point she was cried out and able to talk. "When I got to his apartment, he was leaving with some blonde. I left the cookies by his door, and we came home. If he's dating, there's no use in trying."

Aunt Mel squeezed her hand. "Are you sure? Do you know what was going on?"

"No, but I wasn't hepped about the trip to begin with. And I don't need to catch him with another girl."

"I understand. But there's more to this story than what you're sharing."

Thea searched her face.

Just then the kitchen lights blazed. "What's going on? Thea, why are you home?" Beau rubbed a palm over his scruff.

Great, now she'd wakened him, and he had to get up so early. "Everything's okay, Beau. I'll explain in the morning. Go back to bed."

He didn't argue but turned around and padded up the stairs.

Aunt Mel smiled at her and patted her hand. "Where were we? Yes, you were about unload what you've been harboring."

The denial was on her lips when Thea overwhelmingly needed to tell someone how she'd gotten to this point. Connie said she'd been putting up walls. Well, maybe she'd take down one or two. "I always believed that somehow Phil and I would work this out. But he didn't contact me for so long, I had given up. It was better that way, anyway." She sighed. "He approached me at the wedding, claimed he wanted to be friends. Then he ran away again. Connie helped and now here we are."

"That's not what I mean. What happened to you two? Your mom didn't understand."

She stared at the floor. "I couldn't tell Mom. She'd, well, it would hurt her."

"How?"

"Phil proposed, and I said no." She glanced up and caught her aunt's gaze. "Connie told me he was going to propose. She'd seen him at the jewelers. I planned to say yes, and then we found Mom when she'd had her stroke. How was I to leave her? There was no one else to care for her. He made suggestions, but none of them would work. Then he left for Penn. I never spoke with him again until the wedding." She waited for Aunt Mel to say something, do something to show she understood. But she didn't.

"If you love him, why tell him no? Could it be that he thinks you don't love him as much as he loves you?"

She opened her mouth to answer but nothing came out. Her brain refused to form a response.

"Theodora Joy, I can see you love him. And he loves you or he wouldn't have proposed. It sounds to me like he's still in pain from your refusal."

"That's why he's dating?"

"Who says he's dating? She might be a study buddy. A friend giving him a ride somewhere. Right now, you only see your pain. Why did you tell him no?"

"I had no choice, Aunt Mel. Mom needed me. No one could tell us what to expect for her future, if she'd even come home. What right did I have to leave?"

"What right? That's a funny way to express it. It's not a right to love someone, and it's not a duty either. It is a privilege, a gift. Would your mom want you to turn your back on your happiness for her?"

"She needed me. She needs me."

"Yes honey, she needed you. But now you have help. You can

have a life too." Aunt Mel hugged her. "Don't push love away to be noble."

"What if something happens to Mom?"

"Something will, someday. It will to all of us one day. It's part of God's plan. The fact that your parents had you that much after Beau meant they really doted on you, but having older parents also means you'll more likely get less time with them. It was hard to lose your dad. Loss is never easy, believe me. But you can't let that fear keep you from living." Her aunt was the one person who could tell her that with certainty after losing both sons and her husband earlier this year.

"You think that's what I've done?"

Aunt Mel nodded.

"Connie said I'd been putting up walls, and that's why Phil backed away." She wiped her sleeve under her nose.

Aunt Mel handed her a tissue from her pocket. "I don't know if she's right, but it's a good assumption. What do you plan to do?"

Thea closed her eyes a moment. "I'm going upstairs to bed and pray. I've been doing this in my own power. Now I need God's plan."

"That's my girl."

Thea turned and then thought beyond herself. "Why are you up?"

Aunt Mel smiled. "I'll let you in on something. I told your mother but haven't had a chance to tell Hien. Beau brought the mail over this afternoon from my house, and I had a letter from Lai, Charlie's wife…widow. Looks like I'm a grandmother."

Thea embraced her aunt. "That's wonderful news! Boy? Girl? Tell me."

"Well, Lai said she didn't want to get anyone's hopes raised until she delivered in case anything happened. But Hung Charles Wheaten was born October twenty-fifth. She sent me a picture." She pulled an airmail envelope from her robe pocket and withdrew a photo. "My grandson." A tear tickled.

"You will see him one of these days. You will."

Her aunt kissed her cheek. "Thank you. Sweet dreams, dear heart. May you have a plan come morning."

They hugged, and Thea took her bag to her room. Once in there with her door closed, she changed to her pajamas and pulled out her Bible. She opened to the Psalms. Most verses in that book spoke about evil plans and how the Lord could thwart them. But then she came to chapter twenty.

> *The Lord hear thee in the day of trouble; the name of the God of Jacob defend thee;*
>
> *Send thee help from the sanctuary, and strengthen thee out of Zion;*
>
> *Remember all thy offerings, and accept thy burnt sacrifice; Selah.*
>
> *Grant thee according to thine own heart, and fulfill all thy counsel.*
>
> *We will rejoice in thy salvation, and in the name of our God we will set up our banners: the Lord fulfill all thy petitions.*
>
> *Now know I that the Lord saveth his anointed; he will hear him from his holy heaven with the saving strength of his right hand.*
>
> *Some trust in chariots, and some in horses: but we will remember the name of the Lord our God.*
>
> *They are_brought down and fallen: but we are risen, and stand upright.*
>
> *Save, Lord: let the king hear us when we call.*

Some trust in chariots and horses. She chuckled. Right, some trust in cookies too. But no more. She would trust in God. And she would do whatever He led her to do. If she knew what that was. *The Lord fulfill all thy petitions. Yes, please Lord.*

She put her Bible on her nightstand and switched off the light, praying for Aunt Mel and that she would dream of a solution to this whole mess.

PHIL PARKED HIS CAR, grabbed his backpack from the back seat, and ran to get Karen's door. He hoped she would enjoy the outing though it was getting nippy and they needed to bundle up. "They start over there." He pointed to the sign that showed where a temporary American Revolution fort still had remains on Fort Hill.

She slipped her gloved hand in his.

It warmed his entire body. His fingers curled around hers, and he led her up the hill. The stories of this site filled his mind, and he shared how General Washington had hoped for a more direct battle. How the American losses were a little more but when you factored in the British deserters, their losses were far higher. How Daniel Morgan had brought his men south to Washington after the victory at Saratoga. He was so wrapped up in his sharing, he missed when he lost her attention. It got awful quiet.

She shivered, no longer holding his hand.

"I'm sorry, I get carried away. Would you like something to drink?"

"Yes, I spotted a little place."

"No need of that." He slipped off his backpack and removed a thermos with two cups. "I've coffee." He poured her a cup and handed it over. "Here."

She took it and bought it to her face, the steam rising from the hot liquid.

"Do you use cream or sugar?"

"You've got that in there?"

He smiled and pulled out a second thermos. "Here's the cream. It's milk, but it works. And I have a few sugar cubes in this box." He opened the lid and held it out.

She shook her head but helped herself to two cubes. Then held out her cup for some milk. "You must've been a Boy Scout. Always prepared."

"Nope, I was a farm boy. We have to be prepared too."

"Do you have a blanket in that pack of yours?" She flashed those green eyes that were so unreadable.

"Actually, I do. I'll spread it on that bench, and we can huddle together until you get warmer."

"Good idea." She stood, allowing him to do all the labor. When ready, he presented the double throne. "You do excellent work, sir." She sat.

"Thank you, m'lady." He plopped next to her, and she cuddled in close, pulling her side of the blanket over them. He suddenly wondered if he needed a blanket or a winter coat at all. "Getting warmer?" He sure was.

"Uh hum." She snuggled closer.

"Uh, so, you wanted to talk about your goals today."

She sighed. "I said that, didn't I?"

"Yes, you did."

She sat back. "I do not date for mere pleasure. If I am dating someone, it is to see if we are suitable for a deeper rapport. I think we have some compatibility points, and I'd like to investigate. We need to know each other better. I want someone willing to think in terms of building a life together, exploring a relationship with that in mind. We might not be compatible. But if that's our goal, we don't need all those flirty games. Does that make sense?"

It did. "Yeah. I've never been one to date around. I want to complete my doctorate before I get serious. I learned the hard way. But, if things progress and you're willing to wait, we can see what develops. Is that what you wanted to hear?"

She snuggled in again and nodded against his chest.

He wrapped his arm about her and wondered how it would be to make plans with her, to hold her this way all the time, to kiss her. Thea's face flitted through his thoughts, and he stiffened.

She pulled back. "What's the matter?"

He shook his head. There was no explaining, especially the guilt accusing him.

She settled in again, warming him to the toasty level.

"You know what gets me excited. I mean, look around." He waved his free arm indicating the site. "What gets you excited?"

"Right now, this. I'm content."

He chewed the inside of his cheek. "Glad of that. But I'd like to know your favorite color, what music you like, who you respect. Tell me about your faith."

"My favorite color is purple, I dig the Beatles and I respect you. I attend services with my parents on Sundays, raised in the church. And Neapolitan is my favorite ice cream. I threw that in as a freebie. What's yours?"

He had to think about that. "I guess I'm a plain old vanilla guy. If you start with that, you can add anything you want. I'm a fan of hot fudge sundaes."

She pulled back again. "I think I could have guessed that. Would you like to kiss me?"

He needed to get used to Karen's shock tendencies. "Yes. I would." Since she asked.

"Then what are you waiting for?"

He leaned in, starting soft.

She slid her fingers behind his head and pulled him closer, deepening the kiss. It made his heart race. It also made him feel very wrong.

He pulled back, rolling his lips over his teeth. "Uh, let's walk some more."

She glanced up at him, her eyes squinted as if she'd analyzed what he did.

Truth be told, he wasn't sure why he pulled away. It just felt wrong.

She slipped her hand in his. "Sure, let's walk." She stood, letting go to help him fold the blanket and return it to the backpack. The coffee grew chilled, so they tossed it in what was left of the grass. Then she laced her fingers with his again.

They followed the trail signs to find the Emlan House where Washington had his headquarters during their encampment and the battle of White Marsh. It had undergone some renovation in 1854. Some called it destructive modernization. But the building still stood, and they checked it out.

However, he could tell Karen had lost interest. If she'd had any to begin with. He suggested they return to the car. Once in, he had a nagging inkling he needed to address one more thing. "Karen, I'm sure you're aware that a professor working on his doctorate does not make a lot of money. That is another reason I want to wait to get serious until after I have my degree. I'd like to take you to dinner and events, but I don't have the cash to do that. I'm being honest since you kind of set that tone. No games. I'm happy to do stuff together, but please do not expect lots of dates that require I pay. I'm sorry."

She didn't flinch. "I have money."

He did. "I figured you do, but that doesn't change things. I won't let you pay if we date. The gift of game tickets was one thing. You buying dinner and all is another. I hope you understand."

She nodded. "If that's how you want it. See I have another reason to respect you. You aren't out to take advantage of me."

Had she worried about that? "No, of course I'm not. Karen, you can trust me."

"Good thing, because I do trust you. Okay, I'll let you pay and figure out what your budget can handle. I'll just enjoy learning about you." She smiled.

And he heard in his head, as if Thea whispered in his ear, *"Will you walk into my parlor," said the spider to the fly.*

SIX

Over You

Saturday morning, December 21, 1968

CONNIE LEANED ON HER ELBOWS AT THE KITCHEN TABLE. "He came home yesterday."

"If he wants to talk to me, he knows where to find me." Thea wiped her counters for the umpteenth time. "Listen, Connie, I've prayed about this. My sending him cookies was okay, but putting myself out there more isn't the right move. I'm relying on God for my plan. He knows what I should do. I'll wait to hear what that is."

"Well, perhaps you need to lay out a fleece."

"What?" Thea stopped wiping and turned to her friend.

"You know, a fleece, like Gideon."

"I'm aware of what a fleece is in the Bible. Tell me what you mean. How does this apply to me?"

"Your question is if you and Phil have a future. Right?"

"Yeah."

"So, this a Leap Year. All year long. Until midnight New Year's Eve. You can ask him."

Thea gasped. "I can what?"

Connie hopped up from her chair and stood in front of her.

"You remind him it is Leap Year. Tell him you'd like more than friendship. Then ask him to marry you. If he says yes, all's good. If he says he'd rather do the proposing, still good. If he says no, then you know what your answer is. You move on. No more wishin' or hopin' or plannin' or dreamin'. It's in the open. You can deal with it."

Thea turned away, her view out the kitchen window glistened where a dusting of snow made everything bright in the morning sun. She rubbed her hands over her face. Was this the plan she'd been praying for? She'd certainly get her answer. "What do I need to do?"

She and Connie had rehearsed this while she baked another batch of oatmeal chocolate chip cookies. Then she got ready, Connie picking out her outfit and doing her makeup and hair. She needed no blusher, that was certain. Her cheeks beamed bright pink all on their own.

Three hours later, Thea pulled up in front of Phil's dad's house. Her hands had never shaken so, not even when she brought him cookies to Pennsylvania. Her chest tightened, and her thoughts scrambled.

She smoothed her cream, tan-and-blue plaid skirt Connie had paired with her sapphire angora sweater. The only jewelry she wore was a simple pearl on a chain, a gift from Phil when she graduated from Valparaiso. She hoped he remembered. She hoped he remembered a lot of things.

The box of cookies sat on the passenger side. She wiped her hands over her skirt and swiped them up, climbing from the Tank before she could change her mind.

A curtain at the living room picture window moved. Someone noticed she'd stopped.

Would that someone be glad?

She climbed the steps to the porch, reciting the plan once more in her head. The front door pulled open, and Mr. Carpenter stood there grinning at her. "Thea, so good to see you. What's the occasion?"

She pulled in one more breath. "Well, I was baking. Thought you could use some cookies. 'Tis the season." She winked, trying for easy-going.

"That it is, that it is. But with your cookies, any season is the season. Come on in, sweet girl. Let me take your coat." He had her out of her jacket and seated on the living room sofa before she could think. "I'll call Phil and tell him you're here."

"Thank you." Her mouth was so dry, she didn't recognize her voice.

"Can I get you something to drink?"

She nodded. "Please, water. Thanks."

He yelled up the stairs as he passed, "Phil, you've got company," and then returned with her water seconds later.

She'd taken a swallow when Phil stepped into the room. She couldn't tell if he was happy to see her or uncomfortable or what. He was almost expressionless.

"Hi, Thea. Merry Christmas." He stood, moving as though void of emotion.

"Merry Christmas to you too, Phil. I brought you something." She held out the box.

He didn't take it. Instead he sat on the sofa with her but put plenty of room between them. "What are you doing here?"

So, he wasn't glad to see her. He wasn't angry, though. Confused? "I made you a Christmas present." She held the box out to him again.

This time he took it. "You didn't have to do this."

"I don't give gifts out of obligation. Then they're not gifts."

He smiled at that. "What've you been up to, besides baking?"

"The same old stuff. Taking care of Mom and Beau. Oh, and I've been rehearsing for the Christmas Eve concert. Aunt Mel has stayed with Mom so I can do that. I hadn't sung in so long, I was afraid I had forgotten how, but it's good. I even have a solo."

His smile grew a little sad. Not that his mouth changed, but his eyes held a different light or something. Why would her singing again make him feel bad?

"Maybe I'll get to hear you again. I would enjoy that."

Somehow his words bolstered her confidence. Yet the box remained unopened.

She wiped her hands on her skirt again and noticed he'd taken his glasses off. They were both nervous. She didn't feel so alone. "You haven't opened your box."

"Oh, I'll get a cookie after a while. Not hungry at the moment."

Not hungry? For her cookies? Something was definitely wrong. Those things called his name as if they were his mother. If he was turning down an oatmeal chocolate chip cookie, things could go south quick. "Are you sure? You usually like them, and they are fresh out of the oven. Just the way…" She trailed off as he continued to polish his lenses. She needed to get him to open the box. Everything depended on that.

He finally stopped polishing and put his glasses back on, glancing her way over the top of them before he pushed them higher on his nose.

This wasn't how she'd anticipated this meeting. "You're uncomfortable. I'm sorry." *You're not the only one, Buster.* If he only knew.

"I planned to come see you. Wanted to wait until after Christmas. Give you family time and all." He wouldn't meet her gaze.

"Phil, open the box, please. You don't have to eat a cookie. Just open the box."

Finally, he glanced her way, and she held his gaze. She motioned with her hand, and he unwrapped the package. Her pulse pounded in her ears. She wanted to yell at him to rip the paper off and lift the lid but bit her tongue while he undid the tape, folded the paper and set it aside.

Then came the moment.

He lifted the lid and withdrew the envelope she'd put on top of the cookies. A quick glance her way and then he opened it and slid out the Christmas card.

She watched him read it, knowing every word she had penned.

Dear Phil,

Merry Christmas, or I hope it will be for both of us. When we reconnected at Connie and Jerry's wedding, it was so hard and yet it was the best thing that has happened to me. You rocked my safe little world and reminded me what it was like to be in love with life. Since last August, I've been able to knock down some of the protective walls I'd built around me. I want to keep them down and laugh and love again. I am doing that. I want to do more of it. One thing has become clear. I want you in my life, and I want to be a part of yours. Not casually. Not as only a friend. I was so lost when you were gone and am so grateful you took that first step last August.

I am reminded that things are different with a Leap Year. It has emboldened me to try a Leap Year tradition. You know I am not one to be assertive. But I love you, Phil. I always have and always will. If you are ready to see what tradition I'm attempting, look my way.

He lowered the card and glanced at her as a knock sounded at the door.

That was her cue. Thea slid from the couch to her knees in front of him and reached for his hand as a tear escaped down her cheek. Great, she was getting all sniffly. But this was it. She inhaled, prayed, and exhaled as his eyes grew enormous. "Philip Carpenter. I love you with my whole heart. Will you please marry me, Phil?"

"What are you doing here?" Karen charged into the living room and grabbed Thea by her arm while Phil remained rooted, frozen. "I said, what are you doing here? You have no business being here with my boyfriend."

"I want to go home. May I please have my coat?" Thea stood and glanced around. "Excuse me." She tried to step past, but Karen blocked her. "Please let me pass."

"You think you are so smart, sneaking in while he's here? Like I wouldn't know? I saw you standing in the road, watching like some little waif, and I'm here to tell you, you can forget it. Your pitiful expressions and dropping in whenever the notion strikes is done. He is with me now, and we have plans. He is meant for bigger things than this hick town or old hick girl-friends. So, keep your clutches off my man."

Oh, wow. Thea delivered those cookies in person?

Thea pushed past, grabbed her coat, and raced out the door.

Phil followed. "Thea!"

But she jumped in her car and drove off.

He stepped back into the house to see Karen watched while a cold smile curled her lips.

Phil could tell the second she noticed his shock. Her eyes grew wide, and she gnawed her bottom lip. Then she pasted a big-bad-wolf grin on her face. Like he hadn't seen a thing.

"Hey you! Thought I'd surprise you. Merry Christmas!"

He stayed silent. Never in a million years could he have imagined this. If she had a brain in her head, she wouldn't try to deny what just happened.

"Guess I ran off your company."

"You guess? What are you doing here?" A veil ripped away. He saw behind the curtain to the genuine person, to the things that hadn't set right with him. He didn't like the view.

"I told you. I wanted to surprise you for Christmas."

She did that and more. "Where are you staying? You don't have friends around here, and there's no motel in Breadville." As the shock ebbed away he started to seethe.

"I thought I'd stay with you, get acquainted with your family." She blinked at him. All he saw was pretentiousness.

"That wouldn't work. It's only my dad and me here. In this little hick town." He rubbed that in.

"So, you heard."

"I was standing in the room. Did you think I wouldn't?"

"Well, I'm glad. You needed to be shown what kind of person she is. I must protect my interest and will not have another woman catting around with what's mine."

"What's yours? I don't belong to you. I'm not something you own. The idea was we might build a relationship. Being rude—no, make that cruel—to someone who…means a lot to me? That's not how to find compatibility."

She stared at her feet a moment. When she raised her head, there were tears in her eyes, and she wore a little pout. "I'm sorry. No idea what came over me. I just couldn't stand losing you. I guess I have a tiny jealous streak." She put her hand on his chest and wiggled her fingers up to his hairline. "Might we sit and discuss this?"

He grabbed her hands and pulled them from his face, holding them to her sides. The thought of her touching him made him shiver and not with delight. With a glance about the room, he realized he didn't want her in his house. He didn't even want to introduce her to his dad though they must have met when he let her in the door.

"No. I don't think so."

"Then what will I do?" She blinked her eyes.

It embarrassed him that he'd considered dating her. She wasn't jealous. She was malicious. And the sooner she was gone, the better he'd feel. He needed to gargle, get the thought of her kiss out of his head. But…

"It's too late for you to drive all the way back, so I will make reservations for you at the Howard Johnson's on US 31 in Kokomo. Look at your map. You drove past it when you came. I'll pay for one night. But you need to go home."

It was as if she grew. Her back straightened and her eyes turned icy. "You don't know what you are saying."

"Actually, I do. For the first time in more than a year, I know what I am saying and what I want. And I want you to leave. Your reservation will be waiting for you when you get there."

Her eyes narrowed to slits. Words he had only seen scrawled on bathroom walls geysered from lips he'd once kissed. She ran down the steps to her car, slammed it into gear, and tossed up gravel as she went out the way she'd come in.

When her taillights disappeared at the end of the drive, he closed the door. His dad waited in the living room.

"Want to tell me about it, son?"

Phil nodded. He really did. But first he needed to call the Hojo's as he promised.

Five minutes later he poured it all out to his dad, who had been eavesdropping on Thea's visit but had never even heard of Karen before this moment. The fact that he hadn't said a word to his dad about her was telling.

"She's the dean's daughter and is different. Very straightforward, speaks her mind. It disoriented me, I guess is the best way to say it. I sort of liked how she took control at first but I'd planned to get my head clear here at home. If I couldn't have Thea, I really didn't want a substitute, and Karen made a poor one at that. I just didn't realize she had me mounted on her mantle like a trophy or something. Some kind of possession. Not that I'm any prize. Ask Thea."

Dad snorted at that.

"But I agreed to consider relationship with Karen, before I came back. That's what's had me so out of sorts. She didn't compare to Thea. At first that was good because I thought different would help. But my heart only wants one girl and I figured I'd never have another chance with her. Then tonight... Thea really did that?"

Dad grinned. "She's one in a million, son, and I think you can see she loves you."

"But I never answered Thea. I was in shock from her when Karen burst in. I don't think I could have said a word if she'd allowed it."

"I wouldn't write Thea off yet. You two have a way of getting your timing off. Go to her. Don't give up. You love each other. I'll be praying. It'll work out."

"Thanks Dad, but what do I say?"

"Tell her you sent her Karen packing. Ask her for another try."

Phil sighed. Perhaps if Dad was praying, he'd have a chance. First he needed something. He ran up to his room and rummaged for that velvet box. Maybe he ought to pray, too, for a different outcome. Dad was right about the timing thing. *Please, Lord, work out the timing.*

SEVEN

Reach out in the Darkness

Saturday evening, December 21, 1968

THEA HAD ASKED FOR AN ANSWER. NOW SHE HAD ONE. AND it crushed the last spark of hope. It was over, and all she wanted was to crawl into her room and hide until she could get past her humiliation. It would have been worth it had he said yes. But that there was another? And to have that other dismember her like a chicken en route for the fryer. The salt poured into her open wounds still burned.

Healing would take a lot longer.

This time.

If she ever healed.

She turned into their drive, hoping no one would be around. An ambulance was headed out.

Beau met her at the car before she parked. "It's Mom." Ice crept up Thea's veins. "They're taking her to Howard County Community. Jump in the truck with me. It will be faster."

She followed him at a sprint, refusing to even imagine anything until she was inside the truck and they flew down the road.

Aunt Mel sat in the middle, riding with them, wringing her hands. "They wouldn't let me ride with her."

"What happened?" Thea had to know.

Beau's knuckles were white on the steering wheel. "They think it's another stroke. No one is sure. Melanie called me at the café where I was meeting Jerry. She said you had gone out. I told her to call for an ambulance and raced home. I arrived a minute before you, so I can't add more."

Aunt Mel stared straight ahead. "We were watching the news when she made this funny sound. Her eyes moved like she had no control. I tried to talk to her, but she couldn't respond. Something wasn't right, so I called Beau. Then I dialed for the ambulance and notified her doctor. It all happened so fast."

Thea's walls rose. "I shouldn't have left. It's all my fault. I shouldn't have taken the car."

Aunt Mel patted her leg, but no one disagreed with her. They rode in silence the rest of the way.

Beau let Aunt Mel and Thea off in front of the emergency entrance, leaving for the parking lot.

Thea clung to her aunt's hand and allowed her to lead to the desk. "We're here for Valerie Salem. An ambulance brought her."

"I'll tell them." The nurse was efficient, keeping her word but not sparing a syllable.

It took twenty minutes before they allowed them to Mom's room. Beau had arrived.

Mom was quiet, appeared to be sleeping. Across the hall, chairs clustered in a close alcove. That's where they waited for the doctor or news or anything.

It was like the last time. Same hallway. Same waiting. Same guilt. Again, she'd been elsewhere when her mother needed her. Again, she was thinking of her own happiness and love life. Again, this was all her fault. It was a good thing her proposal didn't work out. She couldn't marry Phil.

Aunt Mel never released her hand, and for that she was

grateful. Yet even with that gesture, she remained alone. Guilt did that. And she was guilty. And selfish. And thoughtless.

"Miss Salem, Mr. Salem?"

The three of them stood as the doctor approached. Beau introduced Aunt Mel.

"Well, your mother had a transient ischemic attack, what we call a TIA or a mini-stroke. This is an expected possibility. It doesn't always happen, but it is common, especially in the first five years after a stroke. The good news is they can pass and often without more damage. Right now, your mother is resting. We'll keep her overnight to be sure, but you might take her home in the morning."

"Thank you, Doctor." Beau shook his hand.

Aunt Mel tapped his arm. "Doctor, may I ask you something?"

"Of course."

"You've been treating Val through all of this, correct?"

"Yes, ma'am."

"Was there anything foreseeable to prevent this? Or the last one?"

"You mean like diet or exercise?"

She shook her head. "No, I mean like proximity. Could someone have stopped this if help arrived sooner?"

"No. What saved your mother's life last time was her robust health. It's hard to be forewarned because the first symptom of stroke is a stroke. These things go undetected. There's nothing you can do except get help. You all did that."

Aunt Mel grabbed Thea's arm and pulled her in front of the doctor. "Then please tell her that. She thinks she's responsible."

"Aunt Mel, please!"

"It's true. You've been feeling so guilty that you've kept yourself from having a life of your own. Your mother knows this, and you can expect her to tell you the same thing when she wakes."

The doctor cleared his throat. "She's right, Miss Salem. You are not responsible in the least. It's evident you've given your mother wonderful care. She tells me about all you do for her at each of our visits."

Her aunt pulled her close as the doctor left. "Let go of that guilt. You didn't make things worse. If anything, you've made them better. It's time you had your own life."

"Oh, Aunt Mel." She wrapped her arms about her aunt and sobbed on her shoulder.

Beau patted her head and said something about coffee.

She pulled back and sniffed. "He can't handle my tears." It made her chuckle. Her big brother, the helping-est person alive. He'd do anything for you but couldn't stand tears or emotional scenes. Right now, it was silly.

They returned to their chairs, and Aunt Mel handed her a tissue.

"His girlfriend came over." How did she admit that without falling apart?

"Girlfriend?"

"He's started another relationship. She doesn't like me very much."

"What gives you that idea?"

"It's a hunch. She told me in no uncertain terms that Phil is her man and that she was taking him from this hick town and his old hick girlfriend."

"She said what?"

Thea nodded. "Yup. I never want to see another oatmeal chocolate chip cookie for the rest of my life."

"I hope you don't mean that."

"Why?"

"Turn around."

She did.

Phil stepped from the elevator.

She stood as he rushed up.

"I'm so sorry."

"Phil, how did you know?"

Aunt Mel spoke in her ear. "Remember, I knew that's where you went. You hadn't come home yet. So, I called and told Mr. Carpenter. He said Phil just ran out the door and that he would try to catch him."

"So, you knew?"

She shook her head. "No, but I figured something happened when I saw your lights turn into the driveway as I hung up. We had things on our minds, so I didn't have time to ask." She patted Thea's shoulder. "I think I will go check on your mother. Why don't you have another talk?"

Thea wanted to grab her, make her stay, but if she was going to face truths tonight, she might as well face Phil Carpenter. "Thank you for coming."

He motioned for her to sit and took Aunt Mel's chair. "I was on my way to your house when Dad got that call."

"Why?"

"To apologize."

"You didn't do anything." Her thumbnail rose to her teeth, but she caught herself and laced her fingers together to stay in control.

"Exactly. I should've stopped her but it all happened so fast. Strangest thing, I heard Karen, and it opened my eyes. First time I really saw her. She was always so assertive, and it was different." He shrugged. "I kind of liked it a little. But when she tore into you and you just took it, it shocked me. Then I wanted to throttle her. I raced after you but you drove off."

"I'm sorry I messed things up for you."

"I'm not. I saw her true colors. I sent her away."

"You did?"

He nodded. "I know you have no reason to trust me, but I'd like to spend some time with you while I'm home to see where this goes."

She searched for that tissue from Aunt Mel because she desperately needed it. "Oh, um, I uh…"

"What is it, Thea? Am I too late?"

"Do you have a handkerchief? I'm going to cry. Again."

"Aw, Thea." He pulled her into his arms, holding her like she'd wanted to be held for a very long time.

FINALLY, something so right in his life. This was what he'd missed. Pulling her closer, Phil bumped the box in his pocket. This wasn't the time or place. He'd tried that before and look where that led them. No, he would wait until things resumed that peaceful rhythm of being with Thea. Like it was supposed to be. For now, he'd hold his girl and offer all his support.

His girl. Thea was, now and always, his girl. He realized that for certain. He only wished he hadn't been so stupid and missed out on having her in his life for a year and a half.

"I'm afraid to let go."

He stroked her hair. "Not going anywhere. I've nowhere else to be."

She relaxed against him, a sweetness that rivaled her best cookies. They remained like that, him holding her while they sat in the alcove's chairs, until the charge nurse told them it was time to leave.

"I didn't get to talk to Mom." She turned to the nurse. "Please, might I?"

The nurse nodded. "But only a moment."

Thea agreed and entered her mother's room, standing in the doorway. He'd no clue from her back whether they spoke or what. Mrs. Wheaten was still in there, and when the women exited, Beau followed, as well. "Hey, Phil, thanks for coming. She'll be okay, or at least okay for her."

"Glad to hear that. Beau, I'd like to drive Thea home, if you don't mind." He glanced at her. "I know you've got family things to discuss but..."

"What do you say, Thea?" Her big brother grinned.

She smiled and sent tingles to his heart. "I'd like that."

They all headed to the elevator where, somehow, Thea's fingers interlaced with his.

In the lobby, Mrs. Wheaten kissed Thea's cheek. "I'll call you tomorrow. Beau'll drop me off. Another excuse to see Hien, I'm afraid." She winked.

"Aw, Aunt Mel, you're on to me." Beau grinned again. "We're parked this way."

It was the opposite direction from where Phil left his car. They said their good nights, and he led Thea to his Impala. It never was slumming when Thea rode in it. Rather she added some class. She snuggled close, and he drove one handed, embracing her with his other arm.

"It's like something dropped into place."

He nodded. Exactly.

"When we arrive, would you like to come in? Beau'll be back in a bit, but it'll give us time to talk."

"I'd like that." As amazing as this felt, and amazing only scratched the surface, they needed to talk. Needed to be on the same page. This time. But until they reached her house, having her close was a gift.

They arrived too soon to suit him, but he was ready for forever. He helped her from his car and walked her to the door.

She flipped on the lights. "Would you like some coffee, or I can make hot cocoa."

No contest. Her hot cocoa was as legendary as her cookies. "Cocoa, please."

She set the cookie jar near him while she mixed her decadent concoction. His gaze followed her every move. He'd come home again. There was no need to talk. He just studied her moves, reveling in the comfort of familiar. Why had he ever walked away?

They'd hurt each other. Unintentionally, but still. He better understood why she referred to him as her friend. It wasn't to put him in his place. And he saw how his moving out of her world without saying anything caused confusion and pain for her. Her words, his actions, pushing each other's buttons. They had to get this in the open before they moved forward.

Soon enough she poured two mugs and pulled up a kitchen chair next to him.

"It's as delicious as ever. Thank you."

She smiled and fireworks went off in his brain.

He needed to garner a little control at least. "Thea, we have to talk about what happened, back when your mom had the stroke. That is where things changed. If we understand what happened for each of us, then we can move forward. I really want to—move forward and understand."

"Me too." She took a cookie from the jar.

"Do you remember at the hospital? When I proposed? My timing was stupid. I get that now. You want me to tell you why I disappeared? Why I didn't call? It was because of what you said."

"What did I say?" Her voice sounded so small, so lost.

"You introduced me as your friend to the doctor. I asked you to marry me, and you called me a friend. I told you words are important. That crushed me."

"But that's what I needed. I needed you to listen and tell me it was going to be all right. I needed you. I still do." She pierced him with her gaze, and it ripped his heart.

He could tell she was about to share something important, that she chose her words. "When Mom had her stroke, I wasn't home. I was at the café with Connie. She had seen you at the jewelry store. I was so excited, trying to decide what I'd wear. I couldn't wait to say yes. But when I got home, I found Mom on the floor. Until tonight, I've been convinced that I somehow caused her to not fully recover because she wasn't found quick enough." She wiped her eyes with her palm, so he offered his handkerchief.

"When I got home tonight, the ambulance was leaving, and I knew I'd messed up again. Aunt Mel figured what I was thinking. She made the doctor explain that I didn't cause any of the stroke effects by my neglect. My head has accepted this, but I still have some guilty pangs. It's fresh, but I'm working on it."

"You thought you were to blame?"

She nodded. "I guess it sounds silly when you say it out loud, but if I'd been home instead of stopping to talk with Connie, I'd have helped her in time, and she wouldn't be so symptomatic."

"That's why you pushed me away." It made sense to him. He understood better than ever how poor his timing had been. He'd meant well, but to propose right after she found her mother was, well, dumb.

"Connie said I put up walls, and I guess I did. I didn't want to feel things when I had no future."

"I thought you just didn't love me enough to marry me."

Another tear escaped down her cheek. "Phil, saying no was the hardest thing I'd ever done, until tonight."

He pulled her closer and kissed her forehead.

She tipped her head to meet his gaze, open and honest. No shock value. This woman he wanted to kiss. No question.

He ran a finger down the side of her face, catching a teardrop before it dropped from her jaw.

Her eyes sparkled with moisture, her breath sweet with chocolate.

He tipped her chin and lowered his mouth to hers.

She returned his kiss, sweetly, deeply, honestly.

He'd do this the rest of his life.

But he needed to stop. He really needed to stop.

"Thea, I better go. I'm not running out on you. For both of us, I must go. I'll be back tomorrow. You're not getting rid of me again. I promise."

She smiled. "I'll hold you to that. Let me walk you out."

As he opened the back door, Beau's headlights pulled into the drive. His timing had improved. He climbed in his car and rolled down the window. She leaned in, and he kissed her one more time before heading for his house.

There was so much to consider. To plan a wedding, anyway, would make it months down the road. And his dissertation still hung over his head. He needed that out of the way. But if he stayed on course, he could go back to Penn, finish up his degree in time to walk at graduation and then they could set a date. He breathed an easier breath than he had in a year. This morning he'd never have believed this possible, but now, now he knew God was the God of the impossible.

Just as he pulled into the drive, he flashed on the place where Karen had parked her car. Something about that caused a shiver to run up his spine. She left furious. She might make his final semester miserable. But considering what he had waiting at home, he could get through it. It was going to work.

EIGHT

Ain't Nothing Like the Real Thing

Tuesday evening, December 24, 1968

THEA BROUGHT A TRAY OF CHOCOLATE CHIP COOKIES, large marshmallows, and steaming mugs of cocoa and set them before the fireplace. Phil left room on the floor next to him for her. Jerry and Connie sat facing them, and Beau and Hien sat on the end. The couples gathered, enjoying the fire's glow, while logs popped every once in a while. So cozy and peaceful.

They'd attended the four o'clock family Christmas Eve service at church because Mom wouldn't have been able to handle later. Sally Ann sang Thea's solo for the late service. But that was fine because now Thea was here with Phil and her best friends.

Making chocolate chip s'mores at the fireplace sounded fun and a little romantic. It'd been a crazy couple of days leading up to tonight. Besides putting together the menu for tomorrow's dinner, there were gifts to buy or craft and wrap. She'd made Phil's, though there'd been little time. But a professor needed to look the part, so she'd sewed him three new ties. She'd worked hard to keep them from shouting "hick" or handmade, and she was sure no one would have anything like them. Her original plan, a corduroy sport coat with leather patches on the elbows, must wait for his birthday. It was impossible to finish by tomorrow.

Beau grabbed a prong and loaded it with a couple marshmallows to toast. "You are watching an expert now, Hien, so take note. You don't want it too dark or uneven. Just rotate like this."

Hien stared, never taking her gaze off the demonstration.

Thea held back her giggle. Her big brother was a marshmallow himself when it came to Hien. But it was good to see how she pulled him from his old-man routine. Hien make her brother young again.

Jerry offered to toast a marshmallow for Connie, and she nodded. They kept sharing glances, talking with coded eye blinks about some great secret. Thea was happy for her friend, even more so now that there weren't the occasional twinges of jealousy. Not that she had feelings for Jerry, or at least nothing more than friendship, but seeing them united when she felt she'd always be alone used to stir that green-eyed monster. A little. But now her Phil was back, the future was hers to imagine. She squeezed his hand.

"Here, Thea, I've got you one."

Thea held out a cookie to Phil, who put a pronged toasty marshmallow on it. She capped it with a second cookie and squished them together while he pulled the prong out, leaving a second marshmallow on it for him.

"Phil, here, let's do it again. I'll help with yours." They moved as a well-trained team. Like they'd been doing this stuff forever. A riding-your-bike moment. You just didn't forget.

When they each had their s'more, he drew her close. She leaned against him. A scan of the room revealed the other couples in similar positions. She was no longer a third or rather fifth wheel. She belonged.

Jerry cleared his throat. "We've an announcement." He

glanced at Connie and squeezed her hand. "Next June, we'll welcome a new member to our family. We're pregnant."

Quiet cheers went up, they didn't want to disturb Mom.

"We need a toast. I think there's a bottle of Martinelli's sparkling cider in the refrigerator. I'll get it." Beau was up before Thea could move. He always let her do the hostess stuff. What gave?

Minutes later, he returned with a tray of plastic champagne glasses. Rather than passing it, he handed each person a flute. He removed the last two, set the tray aside, and then gave one to Hien before returning to his spot. While holding his glass aloft, he motioned for everyone to follow his example. "To Jerry and Connie, may you enjoy parenthood as much as you do wedded bliss."

They clinked glasses when Connie sat forward and peered. "What's that?"

"What's what?" Jerry glanced where his wife pointed.

"In Hien's glass."

Hien stared into her drink, and her eyes grew wide.

"Would you like me to fish it out for you, Hien?" Beau was on his knees in front of her.

Hien nodded while Beau tipped the glass to the side and pulled out an engagement ring.

"Beau, it'll be all sticky." Thea shook her head. Her brother, attempting romance. She had to give him an E for effort, though.

"I do not care." Hien trembled, gnawing her bottom lip.

"Hien, I think I fell in love with you the moment I first saw you that day in the café. And instead of running for safety, you waited until God could pound it through my thick skull that our age differences had no meaning. You were smart enough not to rush, so we'd truly get to know one another. I believe God healed our wounds when He brought us together and now, I can't imagine my life without you. Will you do me the honor of marrying me?"

"Yes, oh, yes!" She threw herself into his arms.

Beau had never been so giddy.

Thea glanced from one couple to the other. Their lives all moved forward. Those special milestones were being met. Yes, she knew it was a little early to rush things for her and Phil. It had only been days since they'd gotten together. But that green-eyed monster wanted to rear its head again.

Phil squeezed her hand, his voice soft and warm against her. "It's okay. We're on the right path. Our turn will come. Have faith." How did he realize what she needed to hear?

An hour later, Jerry and Connie left. Beau drove Hien home leaving Phil and Thea alone to clean up. Mom slept, so they were quiet. At one point, though, before everyone headed home, they caught her awake, so the group shared their good news, a couple at a time. Beau and Hien's news was no surprise. She told Thea she'd been praying for them since before they started dating.

But now Mom slept, and Phil helped Thea straighten up before he had to leave. She washed, and he dried. Like some old married couple. She loved that thought.

"Listening to the announcements tonight got to you a little, didn't it? I have to admit, it did me too."

She searched his face and saw truth in his words. It warmed her that he understood and felt the same way. "I know."

"We're just getting started again. Some things we won't have to relearn. Some things we will. Timing has always been our downfall. We can't let others rush or dictate what is right for us. I have to leave for Penn in a couple weeks, but I should have my dissertation done before graduation. That'll mean a job offer. Then we'll plan a wedding any way you want. Can you hang in there with me? Will you?"

She nodded because she couldn't speak. He understood. That meant the world.

He pulled her close and whispered in her ear. "I love you,

Thea. I always have, I always will. Please, sweetheart, give me time to do this right. I promise you won't regret it."

How could she refuse him? She'd waited this long, she would wait as long as needed. Mrs. Philip Carpenter may still be down the road, but the journey was getting shorter. She hoped.

CHRISTMAS MORNING DAWNED bright and shiny, as it should for someone in love. Phil experienced a swell of emotion that knocked his logic for a loop. He'd loved Thea before enough to want to marry her, but having lost her and gained her back, he had a better gauge of how much he loved her. And it overwhelmed him.

He dressed and bounded down the stairs. Dad poured a cup of coffee. "Good morning and Merry Christmas, Dad."

"Santa must've been real good to you this year. You are happier than I've seen you in a long while."

"I am, I am. Santa didn't do it. God worked this all out, and I'm happy to give Him all the credit. What's for breakfast?" He poured himself a cup and joined Dad at the table.

"What do you feel like making?"

"You really think Christmas day is the time to suffer with my culinary skills? I mean, you have the hospital's number handy, because you might need it." One more reason he loved Thea. He'd never starve with her, that's for sure.

"If you can boil water, you can make oatmeal. I'll get the goodies for it. How about some pecans, brown sugar, and cinnamon?"

"Throw in some raisins and you've a deal." He rose to get a pan and the canister of oatmeal before he finished his sentence.

The phone rang, so Dad answered it while Phil measured the water, sort of, according to the directions on the back of the box. He guessed how much salt to add by measuring into his hand.

Looked good enough. He dumped it in and dusted his hands over the pot.

"Phil, it's for you."

"Who is it?" Maybe Thea calling to say Merry Christmas? That would be nice.

His dad shook his head, but a serious expression crossed his face.

He accepted the receiver from Dad. "Hello, this is Phil Carpenter."

"Merry Christmas, Phil. I've a gift for you." Karen?

"What do you want, Karen?" A chill slithered his spine. This wasn't good.

"I told you. I have a gift. Don't bother returning to Penn State. I took care of everything. You're fired."

"You don't have the power." She couldn't do that, right?

"No? Hmm. Guess someone should've mentioned that to Daddy, because he just let me do it. You can expect his call tomorrow. He didn't care to mess up your holiday with such unpleasant news. He's a softie that way. But I just knew you'd want to know. See, I have no qualms about ruining things for you. It gives me great pleasure. You have no idea what you threw away. Well, Merry Christmas." And she hung up.

Phil stared at the receiver and blinked. Was this some joke? Without the job, no finished dissertation. No dissertation, no future job to support a wife and family. He pulled his glasses off and rubbed his hand over his face, trying to make sense of this. Karen being vindictive, he understood. Nothing about her wanting to hurt him came as a surprise. But that her father fired him on her say so? What did she tell him? What story did she concoct to call for his dismissal?

The water boiled on the stove. His dad assumed his oatmeal job. Which was a good thing. He needed out to think.

"I'm sorry Dad. I gotta go for a walk." He reached for his jacket on the peg by the door to the mudroom.

"Bad news, son? Talk to me about it."

If there was one man he wanted to talk with, it was his dad. But not at this moment. In this moment he must organize what happened, find order in it. "I will. I need to process this. It makes no sense."

He headed out the back way. The farm had gotten a new dress of white overnight and sparkled with fresh snow. His were the first footsteps to disturb the beauty. Only the day had lost its luster. He'd gone to bed dreaming of a future within reach, and now... He had no clue what happened now. Should he wait for the call from the dean? Should he drive back and plead his case?

If he called first, Karen might intercept it. What if Karen had made up things? Could she have accused him of improper advances? How could he tell Dean D'Albany that his daughter was a liar? He blew on his hands and jammed them in his jacket pockets. So many thoughts pounced through his brain. He'd expected trouble from Karen. When she left, she had a tone that cried doom. But this? Being fired? No questions, no inquiry, no what-is-your-side-Professor-Carpenter? He'd missed something. Something vital.

What happened?

Phil turned and stared at his footsteps. He must retrace them to get home. His doctorate might require the same thing. He'd finished the needed classes last year. The dissertation was all he had left. And it was getting to the final stages. They had approved his outline and the abstract paper. He even had a rough draft of the introduction, conclusion, and references. All that remained was to address his methods and discussion. He was so close. He'd thought it was a light at the end of the tunnel.

Now he wondered if it was an oncoming train headed straight at him. If he changed schools, it would mean retracing his steps back to the beginning. Would he need more classes? Would his work be approved elsewhere? Must he start from scratch? What would it cost him to start over? There wasn't enough savings left.

He paused, and it hit him. There was an even bigger question. One he must answer now.

Today.

He raced for the house and grabbed the phone, dialing by memory. "I need to see you right away. Please meet me at the car."

Ten minutes later he pulled up, and Thea ran from the house. He opened the door for her, and she climbed in. He'd left the motor running to keep the heat going. Still, she rubbed her hands together.

"Merry Christmas." She repeated Karen's words, but with a sincerity in her voice. Her smile beamed, and he longed to kiss that smiling face before he dropped any bombs on her life. But that wouldn't be fair.

"I'm not sure it is. We need to talk." It terrified him that he was about to break her heart. Again. This killed him. He never wanted to hurt her ever.

Worry lines formed between her brows, and she grabbed her right thumb with her left hand. "What's the matter?"

He took a breath and plunged. "I got a call this morning from Karen. She's convinced her father to fire me. He's my dean, my boss. Was. I have no job." Then another thought occurred to him. "Unless she was just trying to scare me to get even. She said her dad will call me tomorrow to make it official." Then he'd know.

"Oh, Phil, I'm so sorry. I was afraid..."

He reached for her hand and rubbed his thumb over the center of her palm. "I could see it in your eyes. It's hard to trust me after what we've been through. But I'm not running out on you. I gotta find a job where I can complete my degree, though. I must. I don't know how much of what I've already completed will be acceptable elsewhere. But, if the dean calls me tomorrow, then I start applying. There's good news. I might discover something closer to home. Penn was an amazing location, but since I have all my data, I should be able to work on it from any school."

"That doesn't sound so bad. We can do this. I'm in this with you." She scooted nearer to him.

He pulled her close. "It means we need to put off plans until I have a job and acceptance secured. Can you hang in there with me?"

"Of course I will." She snuggled against him. That was a relief. He'd been afraid she wouldn't go along with waiting. But now he had to find a position and finish his dissertation. And hope and pray that he didn't have to redo the entire thing. *Please, Lord, don't make me start it all over!*

NINE

Words

Friday afternoon, August 2, 1969

THEA GLANCED AT HER WATCH. WHERE WAS PHIL? EVER since he moved back here, she had to work to get his attention. He'd become so fixated on getting a job that he didn't even realize she existed. Okay, well, perhaps not that bad, but...

Once Dean d'Albany's official phone call came the day after Christmas, Phil followed every lead, applied to every school with a doctoral program for American History. He'd receive letters saying thank you for your interest but not at this time. The first one or two disappointed. After the seventh and eighth rejection, it got personal. She wanted to storm the administrative gates of those hallowed halls and shake a few high and mighties and knock them down a peg. However, Phil vetoed any calls or help on his behalf. He said he'd do it. Somehow.

But each rebuff drove him more into himself. She was afraid she was losing him.

Now it was Hien and Beau's wedding rehearsal. He was a groomsman, and she was a bridesmaid. They'd walk the aisle together. A romantic foretaste. Or it would be if he ever got here. She checked her watch again. "I don't know what's keeping him."

"Well, it's nothing too complicated. We can fill him in when he arrives. But we do need to get started." Pastor Bob, always the practical one.

His wife, Judy Harrington, guided the women, showing them where they would be and what to do.

A friend of Hien's from Saigon, back when she worked for the Press Corp, flew in to walk her down the aisle. A guy named Steve. He was tall and skinny with white blond hair and black horn-rimmed glasses. Hien had been excited to see him, though Beau was a little cautious at first. Now they joked like long-lost buddies. The best part was that he brought Hien's sister-in-law, Lai, and her baby boy Hung along with him as a surprise for Aunt Mel. Their story made Thea realize how petty her own troubles seemed.

"Thea, you follow Connie. Wait until she is halfway down the aisle and then you start."

She nodded and glanced at the front where Beau stood with Jerry and Pastor Bob. Phil should be standing there too.

Once Thea was at her spot, Hien walked forward with Steve. After all her future sister-in-law had suffered and rose above, she deserved this happiness. Thea was thrilled for her and for Beau. He'd been alone too long. She'd never questioned why her brother didn't date. She should have. But now he'd found Hien. And she found him. They had each other.

Where was Phil? She expected him to come running through the doors at any moment. But the moments ticked by, and it never happened.

"Okay, let's try it again and this time, Judy, why don't you play the organ so they can get adjusted to walking with the music."

Thea returned to the narthex door to wait for her cue. They had plans to have dinner at the Breadville Café. That's where Beau and Hien met, so they thought it'd be fun to take over the place for the evening. Of course, with Beau being the owner, it wasn't hard to arrange.

They were so stinking cute, Hien giggling and looking shy. Beau grinning like a big fool.

She wanted a life like that with Phil.

"Thea, it is your turn." Hien tapped her shoulder, returning her to the moment.

When everyone was in place, Pastor Bob explained the order of what would happen so they'd know what to expect. Then they practiced walking back down the aisle. Thea walked alone. She blinked to stop the tears and worry.

"Questions?" Pastor Bob wasn't the least put off being a groomsman short.

"I think we've got it. I'll show Phil what to do. Will he meet us at the café?" Jerry didn't sound concerned.

"Your guess is as good as mine, Jer. I'm keeping my fingers crossed." She held up her crossed digits for emphasis.

"Okeydoke, then. Would you like to ride with us?"

Thank goodness someone thought of that. She hated to ask and appear pitiful. "Yes, please."

Jerry's smile had a little pity in it. Not what she wanted.

Aunt Mel had Mom with her and Lai with Baby Hung. They would meet the wedding party at the café. Now that everyone knew their part, the party could commence.

Margie and Lulu, the waitresses who really ran the place, stayed late to prepare and serve at the festivities. Breaded tenderloin sandwiches all around. They'd even decorated with crepe paper and had Beau's favorite song playing on the jukebox as they walked in—"Good Vibrations." It had the makings of a magical evening crafted for the lovebirds.

Thea wanted to be happy for them, and deep inside she felt their joy, but right now, she fought against fear. Did he get so tunnel-visioned he forgot? Or was he hurt somewhere, and she was in the wrong place again? The fact was, this wasn't typical Phil Carpenter behavior. He was always prompt, and he cared about others. Based on those two facts, she had reason to be afraid.

Thea dug in her purse and found a dime. She used the café's phone by the front door and tried his house. But his dad said he hadn't been home since before noon. After thanking him, she hung up and struggled to think where else she could check.

Beau called everyone over. On the counter behind him sat mugs of root beer floats. "Hien and I want to thank you all for coming and planning to be part of our special day. Back when we first met, I introduced Hien to root beer. After realizing it's not an alcoholic drink," he turned and winked at his almost bride who blushed, causing their guests to giggle, "she told me she tried it to be polite but didn't like it. I promised her then that I would treat her to a root beer float when it warmed up and that she'd enjoy it. I don't think she believed me, but guess what folks, I was right. She became addicted—Ow!" Hien punched his arm. "Thea, did you teach her that?"

Now everyone looked her way and chuckled. Oh, well, it was possible she punched him sometimes. When he deserved it.

"Back to what I was saying, turns out Hien really likes root beer floats. So, we're making a few toasts. Please grab a mug and raise it."

Mugs got passed to all.

"First, to my mother. I know for a fact you prayed for this day. Here's to you, Mom."

Clinks and voices called out "Cheers!"

Hien held up her mug. "And to my Mil. Though, technically Aunt Val will be my mother-in-law, you will always be my Mil, my second mother, and my friend. I love you."

More clinks and cheers.

Beau embraced Hien. "And to all of you who have befriended us, loved us, traveled far, and supported us. Thank you."

Thea caught her brother's gaze as the last round of clicks and cheers reverberated. He worried too. She saw it in his eyes.

People finished eating and they shared bridal party gifts, Margie and Lulu gathered up the dishes, cleaning where they could. More quarters got dropped into the jukebox and couples danced until Beau finally announced they needed to let the girls close up and go home. He thanked everyone for coming and then sidled up next to Thea, assuring her he'd get her to the farm.

Mom was ready to drop, so they had another reason for calling it a night. Once Beau and Thea had Mom in the car, she caught him kissing Hien goodnight. He wouldn't see her again until they met at the altar. They were so in love, it made Thea want to cry.

She held it together for the ride home. Though she expected questions about Phil's no-show performance, none came. Which was worse because then she realized they felt sorry for her.

They got Mom all tucked in, and she fell asleep at once.

Thea was on the third step up to her room when the phone rang. She turned but Beau grabbed it and motioned for her to go on up as he whispered something at the mouthpiece.

Once in her room Thea knelt by her bed. "Lord, You know exactly where Phil is. Please keep him safe and bring him back. I just can't lose him again." She buried her face in her bed and cried.

"But Beau." He turned to his dad. "He won't call her to the phone. Says it's too late and his mom just got to sleep. He's afraid of waking her, especially since tomorrow is such a big day."

"What did you expect? You needed to get word to her a lot sooner."

"Dad, there was no way. I have the best news to tell her and can't get to her."

"Try in the morning."

That was the only plan to make sense. He must reach Thea first thing. But tonight would be better. Oh, he understood. Phil didn't blame Beau, and asking him to tell Thea wouldn't work. He needed her to be the first to hear his news.

It had started out with a trip to Kokomo. He wanted to pick up the gift he'd ordered for Beau and Hien. It wasn't great, but the downtown Sears had a decent choice of nice items. That was where he ran into him.

Him being Dr. Behler of Indiana University Kokomo campus. IUK opened their new site in 1965, but since that move, things continued growing, and their first group of graduates to earn bachelor degrees would walk next year. Phil had seen the man's photo in the newspaper. He had dreams for this IU location.

All well and good. But Phil needed his doctorate. The sooner the better.

Somehow, they struck up a conversation about choosing the best wedding gift. Turned out, Dr. Behler needed one for a different couple. The guy had a knack for drawing things out of a person, and before Phil realized it, he was sharing his life story over a lemonade at Fenn's.

The man listened, really listened. Then he offered hope.

"If you'll give me a copy of your resume, I have an idea. Would you be willing to teach? There's an opening in the history department. And if you are on staff with me, you can do your doctoral studies through the main campus. We're not there yet. But you'd have a foot in the door, since you'd be employed at IUK. I can set you up with an adviser there, and you'd travel to Bloomington once a week to meet. If you scheduled your classes on Tuesday and Thursday with office hours on Mondays and labs on Wednesdays, Fridays would be your Bloomington days."

"What about all my work? Would I have to start from scratch?"

"I'm guessing, since I haven't seen your transcripts, that your classes from Penn will transfer. And, though you'd need to resubmit your thesis statement and outline for approval, if it passed Penn's board, it should pass ours. We both strive for excellence."

"There is one thing." Phil had to spell out why he wasn't at Penn and needed a job. But how did he explain without gossiping about the D'Albany family? "It was not my choice to leave Penn State."

"You were in the history department, right?"

"Yes."

"I know the D'Albanys. In fact, a nephew of mine, the one getting married tomorrow, met Miss D'Albany at a sorority-and-fraternity mixer. He transferred out at the end of the semester. I don't think she counted on him having a family with influence, because she and her father tried to blackball him. Had him labeled as a trouble maker and someone who took advantage of young ladies. I've seen their work. I can't figure out why he lets her do the things he does or why he doesn't question her claims. Once, maybe. Twice? I'd wonder what was going on. However, you are not the first nor second to have the D'Albany treatment."

"They really had me blacklisted? I'd suspected that's why I couldn't get accepted into any program, but it seemed so unbelievable."

Dr. Behler nodded his head. "Let's go to my office. I'll start you on the process."

"Now?"

"That is, if you are interested."

"Yes, I am definitely interested."

Dr. Behler stood. "You need to understand, there's only one opening. Several have applied. I like you, and I think you deserve the chance. That's why I'm giving you a bit of an inside track. But if we don't get this moving, the hiring committee will push for one of those resumes on my desk. You can use my type-writer. Then we'll put in an official request for your transcripts and you should be set."

Phil stared at the man. Who did this? And why at this moment? He needed to reach Thea. but there was no way. She'd headed for the rehearsal. If he left this second, he'd only be a few minutes late. But he'd also be turning down the thing that could give them their future. Now that he comprehended the extent to which Karen had gone to ruin his life, he realized this was his one opportunity. He had to grab ahold. This was it. "May I use your phone at the office? I'll reverse the charges."

"Of course."

"Then let's do this."

They shook hands, and Phil agreed to follow Dr. Behler to his office on the campus. Fifteen minutes later, the man unlocked his door. He pulled out an application, some typing paper and uncovered his IBM Selectric. "Have at it, Mr. Carpenter. I have work to do in my library. The phone is there, punch nine to get out. Holler if you need me." He stepped into an adjoining room.

After getting an outside line, Phil got the operator to place the long-distance call and prayed his dad would accept the charges and then get a message to Thea. Instead it rang and rang. He glanced at his watch. Had he started milking already?

It was time to get busy. Maybe he could try again in a bit. The sooner he did this, the sooner he could get home.

Phil stared at the machine. This was a dream. It had to be. He was going to wake up about the time the paper magically positioned itself between the rollers and began singing out all his accomplishments. He pulled off his glasses and polished them. When he returned them to his face, the application and type-writer were still there. Dream or not, he'd better type.

And that's where he was when he wasn't where he was expected. But when he finished and handed the completed document and resume to Dr. Behler, the man grinned and shook his hand again.

"Last thing. Request of transcripts. I have the paperwork

here. If you fill that out, I will see that it gets to the registrar's office."

"Thank you, sir. You don't know what this means."

Dr. Behler chuckled. "Oh, I've got an idea. Just realize, we are a smaller campus. We're growing but we have a long way to go before we have Penn's budget. I doubt we can offer you the same pay. But we will work with you to help you get that degree. I'm glad we ran into each other."

"Me, too. Thank you, sir."

"I'll be contacting you early next week for you to come sign your contract."

"I look forward to that." And so much more.

Then he left for home, driving faster than he should. As he passed the café on his way through town, the lights were out and he knew, deep in his gut, this was going to be bad. Had he gained his dream only to lose the prize?

At home, Dad told him of Thea's call while he dialed her house before doing anything else.

And he didn't have the chance to explain. How could he make her appreciate his dilemma? He had to. Everything depended on her understanding. If he couldn't get through to her, none of the rest mattered.

She'd always said actions speak louder. Well he'd show her some actions. But then she'd better listen. Really listen.

Thea, you've gotta hear my words.

He climbed the stairs to his room to put the finishing touches to his plan.

TEN

Sealed with a Kiss

Saturday morning, August 3, 1969

THEA PLASTERED A SMILE ON HER FACE. IT WAS HER brother's big day, and he'd waited a very long time for it. She was happy for him, but now more than a little scared about Phil. She needed to hide it, though and not ruin the big guy's special day.

Beau walked in the back door from milking "his girls."

"What can I make you for breakfast?" Thea glanced up.

He appeared pale.

"Is everything okay?"

He nodded. And nodded.

Something wasn't right. "Beau, what is it?"

He sat at the kitchen table. "I guess I'm nervous. Tonight, this'll be Hien's home too. She'll be here, sharing my life, my space, my family. I know this is what I want. But what if I mess this up? What if she sees what a big dope I am? What if she doesn't like being a farmer's wife?"

"Oh, Beau, Hien knows you are a big dope and that you will mess up." She gave him a hug. "Don't you understand? You two were meant for each other. Look at all God did to

101

bring you together, how He prepared the way. She's already seen what our life is like and even has worked on her place planting her garden and running her egg business. Oh, I wanted to ask you, what'll happen with Aunt Mel and their farm?"

"I'm going to join it to ours so it'll be one big spread. Aunt Mel will keep the house as long as she wants it."

"Good. So back to my original question, what do you want for breakfast? It's your day. I'll fix you anything. You name it."

"Anything?"

She nodded.

He grinned. "How about two eggs over easy, French toast, and a bunch of bacon?"

She winked at him. "You got it, brother dear. Eggs, French toast, and bacon coming up. Go check on Mom and see what she'd like while I start yours going, k?"

He headed into the other room while she pulled items from the refrigerator. She was glad for something to do to keep her mind off Phil.

"Mom says scrambled eggs and toast is fine. Two strips of bacon too. Please. Want me to set up trays so we can eat with her?"

"Sure." One last time. The three of them. She loved Hien and looked forward to her living here, but there was something very deep, very original about the two of them eating breakfast with Mom, especially today.

Fifteen minutes later, she plated everything. Beau returned to help carry the dishes and utensils. Thea came back for their coffee mugs.

Her brother needed her to smile and not ruin his day. So she pushed her fear down with a plan to make a call as soon as it wasn't too early.

Mugs in hand, she returned to Mom's room and distributed them.

"Thea, are you okay?"

Beau stared at her. Even on his special day he was looking out for her.

"I'm just a little concerned about Phil. I thought for sure he would have called last night or this morning."

"He did."

She jumped and splashed coffee over her plate. "When? Why didn't you tell me? Is he safe?"

Beau ran a hand over his face. "He called last night, but you'd just gotten Mom to sleep so I told him it was too late, to try today."

"You did what?" Thea slugged him good that time.

"Ow!" Beau rubbed his shoulder. "I'm sorry. You know Mom needs her sleep and how it will be a strain on her today. I should've told you."

"Ya think? I was worried it was too early, but I'm calling now."

"Te-ah, oo nee tah wi im."

"Mom, I know, I've got to talk with him. I'll be back." She raced for the phone only to have his dad say he'd just left. No idea where he was going. Thea hung up as a sob choked her.

Beau put his arm around her. "It's gonna be okay. Give him the chance. I'm sure he'll explain. If his excuse isn't any good, then dump him on his head. Punch his lights out. Whatever. I'll help. All right?"

She didn't want chuckle, but her brother beating up Phil was so out of character, she had to. "I know there has to be a good explanation. I need him." She sighed. "I need a walk." After putting her plate in the sink, she went out the front door to the porch and down the steps.

Her flower garden filled the beds around her house with fragrance and bursts of color. It was where she found freedom to experiment with shades and tones, often gathering ideas she used in her sewing projects. It was also where she could talk with God and see His hand at work. "Father, I am so tired of hurting. I feel so afraid. Thank You for letting me know he's safe. But this is crazy. Each time I glimpse good, something comes and steals the joy. I've hung in there while he sent out his applications. I'm content to not be a professor's wife. I'd be happy to love him if he farmed like his dad or dug ditches or anything. I realize this is his dream, and I'm happy to support it. But please help him find what he needs, Father. I—"

A motor sounded, coming up the drive. She peeked around the house to spot Phil's Impala parked in front of the porch.

She charged toward him. "Where've you been?"

"We need to talk, Thea."

She shook her head. "I believed in you. I waited for you."

"Listen, Thea."

"Please, don't give me words. I've been scared out of my mind."

He grabbed her hand and led her to the front porch. "Thea, you need to hear me. Please."

"I need to see your actions. I needed you to let me know you're safe." She broke. This was too painful.

He grabbed her shoulders. "I called. Beau said it was too late to talk."

"But you could have called earlier. Why didn't you just call?"

"That's what I'm trying to tell you. I tried to call, to get a message to you through my dad but he didn't answer. It was long distance, and I had to reverse the charges at the office—" He pulled her to the swing and made her sit. "Listen, I was at IUK. I spoke with Dr. Behler. I told him the entire story, and he offered me a professorship. He's figured a way to meet most of the perks from Penn. It's not as much money, but I have a job."

She wiped the moisture from her cheeks. What was he saying?

He knelt in front of the swing. "Honey, don't you see? How can I marry you and not support you or our future family? Now I have a job. The goal is in sight—you. You are my goal. You're the reason for my actions. I love you, Thea. Please marry me. Say yes this time."

She threw her arms around his neck falling out of the swing. They landed in a heap together on the porch floor.

"Are you all right, Thea?"

She sobbed hard. All she could do was nod.

"You are okay?"

She nodded.

"And you will marry me?"

She nodded again.

"Not good enough. I've got to hear it." He let her go and sat with his back to the porch railing.

Thea scrambled to sit next to him, running her hands over her eyes. "Phil!"

"I mean it. Say it, or I won't marry you. Words are important."

"C'mon, marry me, Phil! I say yes!"

He pulled her close, and she melted into him.

"One more thing. Let me get into my pocket." He moved her to his side and pulled out a small box. "I never could take this back. I picked it for you. May I put it on your hand?"

"Yes." She wasn't about to risk another nod. With her fingers held out for him and delightful shivers trembling through her, he slipped the ring over her knuckles. "Oh, Phil, I love you so."

He pulled her close, placing a kiss on each eyelid, her nose, each cheek and then her mouth where he lingered, deepening his touch while she answered with her whole heart. He loved her. He wanted to marry her.

And she said yes.

"I now pronounce you man and wife. You may kiss your bride."

Phil watched as Beau lifted Hien's veil. Though his view of Beau's face was blocked, he saw Thea's. Tears dripped down her cheeks, pooling in the corners of her smile. It didn't take much imagination to think about raising her veil and kissing her, their first kiss as man and wife. If he weren't careful, he'd be crying too.

"May I present for the first time, Mr. and Mrs. Beauregard Salem."

The guests applauded while Beau and Hien laced fingers and started down the aisle to the back of the church. Next, Jerry and Connie met at the altar and walked down the aisle too. Now it was his and Thea's turn. Jerry had filled him in on all the details while the guys changed into their tuxes. But his thoughts strayed to how stoked he was to escort this lovely woman today.

The wedding party formed a receiving line in the narthex. Guests would file past, offering congratulations before they moved to the parking lot to drive to the reception, one again hosted at the Casa Grande Restaurant in Kokomo.

Phil, next to Thea, restrained himself as he desperately wanted to drape his arm around her. He glanced at the rest of the line.

Melanie Wheaten stood in for Hien's mother. Her friend Steve, who was a real hoot while they got ready, represented her father. Hien's sister-in-law Lai and her baby Hung were placed next to Mrs. Wheaten. Then came Hien and Beau—the new Mr. and Mrs. Salem—followed by Thea's mother. The brides-maids and groomsmen brought up the rear. They were an odd-looking group, strictly from a small-town Indiana point of view. But the obvious love for each other made it perfectly normal.

Soon the wedding party finished their photos and piled into cars to meet the guests at the restaurant. Through it all, no one asked him where he was yesterday or mentioned Thea's new jewelry. That was fine. They didn't want to steal any limelight from Beau and Hien. After they had time on the porch, Thea wanted to show her mother the ring. Beau was in the barn, so they could talk without him knowing. Together they decided not to say anything, though Thea insisted she wouldn't take the ring off. Now that he'd placed it on her finger, he agreed with her decision. Plus, she said she doubted anyone would note her hand when Hien was the focal point.

But she was wrong. When they walked out of the church, Thea whispered to him that Connie spotted her ring. She made her friend promise to keep it quiet.

Sure, that would happen.

At the reception, he figured out that at least one other person had noticed too. Hien threw her bouquet straight at Thea, who caught it and smiled at him, making his pulse race.

Later, the couples had a moment. They plied him and Thea with questions about when it happened and if had they set a date.

"It happened this morning, and he made me ask him. Not even leap year anymore, and he made me." Thea grinned and winked.

All eyes turned to him. The women appeared shocked, the men impressed.

Phil pulled off his glasses and polished.

Thea took them from him and cleaned the lens before putting them back on his face. "Okay, it wasn't exactly like that, but sort of."

They all laughed.

"But what about the date?" Of course, Connie needed to know.

He caught Thea's glance. She nodded, and he explained. "I have a job at IUK. And I'll be able to finish out my doctorate this next school year. I might get done early, but to be safe, and so we can save up for a down payment for a house, we're considering next May. A year from now. So, keep your calendars clear."

Thea wove her fingers with his as he shared.

Phil leaned in and dropped his voice. "By the way, where did you meet that Steve guy? He's a riot."

Hien smiled. "He helped me many times. I consider him a big brother."

Connie nudged her. "You might want to keep an eye on

your big brother because I just saw him ask Sally Ann Meister to dance."

They all turned where Connie pointed as The Association sang "Cherish."

Phil leaned toward Thea. "Last time we danced to this song, it was rather painful. Think we could try it again?"

She smiled that smile he couldn't resist. "Yes, I'd love to. I think our timing is getting better. "

He led her to the dance floor, drew her close, and whispered, "Thea, I love you so. I always will."

Acknowledgments

First of all, thank you, Lord, for trusting me with another story to tell and all Your help getting it told.

Thank you to my P.I.T. crew who prays me through each and every story—Annie, Deb, Lori D. Julie, Dorothy.

Thank you to my early readers—Mary England, Dorothy Shields, Esther Bailey

Thanks to my Beta Readers and Street Team—you all are the best!

Special thanks to my Pencildancer partners in *rhyme* (okay, I'm trying too hard)—Angie Breidenbach, Diana Brandmeyer, Liz Tolsma, Jen Crosswhite. You are amazing writers and have shared so freely. I can't thank you enough for letting me eat my writing lunch at your table.

Thanks and more thanks to my friend, cohort, and editor/publisher (talk about a partner in crime!) Jennifer Crosswhite. Your friendship grows more dear each day.

Special thanks to my mentor and encourager, Esther Bailey —I thank you each time, but I wouldn't be doing this if it weren't for you. What a blessing you are!

Finally tons of thanks and love to my family for ***still*** hanging in there with me and supporting me. I love you, Phil, Jaime, Jonathan, Alyssa, Juan, Natalia, Meg, Mat, Owen, Mom, Amy, Rick, Rusty, and all my extended loved ones.

And, as always, E.B. I still miss you.

Author's Note

Here we are again, Dear Reader.

Funny, I thought *Relentless Heart* would be a standalone. But one day, driving to church with the oldies station playing, the Fifth Dimension came on singing "Wedding Bell Blues." I was struck by the title as if it were new (and not like I'd heard it for half a century). I knew there was a great, sweet love story there. Imagined it to be light and fun.

And then, Thea came to mind. What if I told her story? What was her story? That took me on a journey to her heart and that of the guy with the wireframe glasses and curl on his forehead. He was first going to be Gary Dean in *Relentless Heart* but when I thought of *Wedding Bell Blues*, he had to be Bill something. But that wouldn't work, too close to the song. So he became Phil Carpenter with a nod to my own farm boy/college professor (mine taught briefly in Upstate New York).

Thea didn't want to be merely a supporting character, and you know those baby-of-the-family types. "If Beau can have his story, I want mine too." I'm glad she pushed me. This was fun.

But coming up next is another full-sized story of Beau's parents. I'm excited for you to see how God pulled another old Bible story out and used it to inspire *Relentless Joy*. It might surprise you. Right now, the release date is set for mid October 2020. But if you want a sneak peek, keep reading.

Until we meet in the next story…

Abundant blessings!

Jenny

Before you go, would you please leave a review? It can be a simple "I loved it!"

About the Author

Jennifer Lynn Cary likes to say you can take the girl out of Indiana, but you can't take the Hoosier out of the girl. Author of The Crockett Chronicles trilogy, she makes her home in Arizona with her husband of forty years where she enjoys sharing her tales of Kokomo with her grandkids.

You can find her at www.jenniferlynncary.com

facebook.com/authorjenniferlynncary

instagram.com/jenny.cary_author

Sneak Peek of Relentless Joy: The Relentless Series Book 3

Prologue

Friday, June 1, 2068

"They're in here." As Cadet Anderson held the door for her, Natalia suddenly wanted to hide. How stupid! She'd landed this prize interview because the last one with this guest went so well. And now her nerves screamed *run*? How crazy was that?

Natalia took a deep breath while her producer encouraged her. "You'll do great. Remember, he requested you. You can do this." The voice in her ear helped. But the tour of the West Point facilities, probably meant to put her at ease, only heightened her awareness of how surrounded she was by tradition.

Inside, five chairs sat in a circle. Five? Should only be four. Oh, well. Maybe they thought she'd have someone with her. But with all the technology and security, she needed no one else to accompany her.

A second later, three men, appearing like the same man at different life stages, entered followed by the ever-present Secret Service detail.

"So glad you could come, Ms. Alaniz." The President of the United States, David Joshua Salem, held out his hand to her. "I want you to meet the men of the hour. My father, Jesse Salem, Superintendent of West Point, and my son, soon-to-be Second Lieutenant David Joshua Salem, Jr. Dad, son, this is Ms. Natalia Alaniz, the remarkable reporter who told Ba's story so well."

Both the superintendent and cadet shook her hand, and the President directed them to the chairs as her knees turned to gelatin.

"Ms. Alaniz, is this your first time at the academy?"

"Yes, it is." Natalia had traced the rules of West Point to 1802 and that initial graduating class of engineers. Two hundred sixty-six years was a lot of steeping in tradition.

No wonder her knees wanted to buckle after viewing Eisenhower Hall, Washington Hall (the cadet mess), and Michie Stadium. And of course, The Plain where tomorrow's graduation ceremony would take place. "Cadet Anderson was a fine tour guide."

Then the door opened again. The men remained standing. "Before we start, we have a surprise." President Salem winked at her.

Natalia glanced at the doorway. It couldn't be. But it was.

Owen Salem, the ninety-eight-year-old grandfather of the President, entered the room. Though he used a cane, he still stood tall, straight. Natalia read in the other men's faces that they would rush to his aid if needed, but out of respect they stayed put, showing him the dignity of coming to them. His smile was warm, and his eyes danced, knowing he'd just pulled something over on this unsuspecting reporter.

Her jaw must be scraping the floor. She resisted the urge to lift her hand beneath her chin, but her producer didn't hold back. "Holey macaroni! Did you know? You've scored an interview with the four Salem men, Natalia! You'll be up for a Pulitzer."

Breathe. You can do this. She inhaled, exhaled, and stepped forward with her palm outstretched. "It is wonderful to meet you, Mr. Salem. Thank you for joining us."

After shaking her hand, Owen Salem took his seat. The others followed suit.

She handed out the tie clips which held the cameras and mics, received the tech check okay from her producer, and got this once-in-a-lifetime interview started.

"I cannot believe I have all four of you here together. Please forgive me if I'm a little star struck." Deep breath. She smiled. "This week is special for your family. Why don't you tell me about it?"

They glanced at each other, mirroring grins that must be standard issue in the Salem tribe. Finally, deferring with respect, President Salem motioned to his father. "Dad, you start."

Jesse Salem cleared his throat. "I will. You're right. This is a first, I believe. Can't recall another instance when the retiring West Point superintendent had a grandson about to be graduated from the Academy." He glanced at the others who shrugged or shook their heads. "It is exciting and bittersweet, as I've enjoyed my tenure."

"And you all can claim West Point as your alma mater. How far back does this go? I don't recall that Beau Salem, your grandfather, attended here."

"No, he didn't. Dad, you need to share this part." The superintendent, Jesse, nodded to his father, Owen.

"My father, Beau, was a farmer. He enlisted and served in the Korean War, though he never wanted a career in the military. But that doesn't make me the first in the family to attend West Point. You knew that, right?"

Natalia shook her head. "No, I thought you were. Who was the first?"

"My grandfather, Jimmy. James Roy Salem, Jr. He wasn't just the first in the family to win an appointment, he was the first in the family to graduate from high school and to attend any type of higher learning center."

She recalled her notes. "He died before you were born, didn't he?"

"Yes, I never met him. But I do remember my grandmother telling me stories."

"That was Val? Valerie Salem?"

Owen nodded, as did the other men.

"What do you know of his military career? Did he serve during a war?"

The men glanced at each other, determining their spokesperson. Owen began. It was his father's story. "He didn't fight overseas. Instead he was part of one of the saddest events on our home soil. Our government against our veterans. Most are unaware of the circumstances. But he made a difference. To me, he is a hero in the very truest sense of the word."

"What happened? What did he do?"

"The first thing he did was win an appointment to West Point and graduate. That alone was a feat."

Chapter 1: My Angel

Friday morning, 25 May 1928

West Point Military Academy

Cadet Jimmy Salem itched to twist and look behind him as the other three classes paraded past his graduating class of Firsties. It was only the second occasion he'd been in this position. The first was upon arrival his plebe year. The other cadets paraded to accept him and his class. Now he and his classmates were honored for completing their time and work. But those he longed to watch him honored weren't in the stands. At least, as far as he noticed without asking for trouble on his next-to-last day in an academy uniform. He hoped that somehow they decided he was worth their traveling all the way from Indiana to New York.

The band finished "Auld Lang Syne" while the long gray line of graduates stood, the first row of honored guests. As Firsties, they were now among the reviewing party.

The last note played, and the other classes marched from the Plain. The festivities kept to a tight schedule, though they allowed room for family gatherings this special day.

If one had a family who cared to attend.

"C'mon, Jimmy, you can go with me and my folks." Ernie Wheaten, his best friend and roommate, understood but would not let him wallow.

"Where to?"

"Mom said she'd like to picnic near the water. We won't have to leave the post. Let's go."

Jimmy followed his buddy and found a smile to smack on his face. No need to make Ernie's family miserable too.

Ernie's folks turned out to be funny and warm like him. Jimmy was certain he'd never have made it through these four years without his roommate. He'd have chucked it all and crawled home with his tail between his legs, the failure his father knew he was.

But Ernie didn't see him as a failure. Jimmy wasn't sure what his friend saw, but whatever it was, it came out as encouragement and loyalty all wrapped up in a funny quip or joke. Or a prayer. He did that too. Ernie was a complex guy, but a grand pal.

"So, Jimmy, I hear you're from Indiana. Where abouts?"

"The central part of the state. I'm from a little place called Breadville. We're about halfway between Peru and Kokomo."

Ernie's dad grinned—now Jimmy saw where his friend's grin came from. "I know that area. Have you ever been to Gibson City?"

"In Illinois? No, but Ernie has told me so much about it, I feel like I've been there." And that was the truth. Ernie loved his old home town. He'd even kept Jimmy up late reminiscing after he'd received a letter from his mom.

"Well, the central Midwest farming area is all pretty similar." Ernie's mom tried to stave off a discussion on Illini versus Hoosier practices.

Jimmy had to laugh. "Bet there's a few farmers who might disagree. My dad has his dry goods store but his brother farms outside of town. Uncle Lyle's place has always been a favorite to visit." The mention of the farm brought back the better hometown memories. Uncle Lyle was the nurturing of the two brothers. He should have just invited his uncle and cousin. They would have come.

Mrs. Wheaten unpacked the picnic lunch and made sure everybody had plenty. "Not as good as I would've fixed in my own kitchen, but not too bad for store bought."

Conversation lulled while everyone ate. Jimmy thought the food was great and tried to imagine how much better Ernie's mom's cooking was.

An hour later, after policing the grounds, they needed to join their fellow cadets at the barracks.

Ernie kissed his parents goodbye, and Jimmy thanked them again for including him. He wanted to add "and for not being too sympathetic" but since they didn't bring it up, why should he?

But back at their room, he raised it with Ernie. "You didn't have to include me, but thanks."

"I couldn't have you walking around here all droopy faced. You'd scare the plebe class. Besides, my parents always wanted another kid. They'll just adopt you." Ernie threw a pillow at him. "See, we're like brothers already."

Jimmy chuckled and tossed the pillow back. He'd easily let Ernie's folks adopt him. "You sure they'd want a Hoosier? I'm not so keen on all that Fighting Illini stuff myself."

"You'd learn to love it." Ernie grabbed his towel and headed for the showers leaving Jimmy alone with his thoughts.

Starting after all the ceremonies and traditions tomorrow, he had thirty days of leave. He'd thought of going home. First time in four years. But if his parents didn't care enough to attend graduation, why should he go back? Could he report early to his post in North Carolina? Or could he take some of his hard-earned money and have a brief vacation? One thing was sure, he wouldn't be seeing Breadville, Indiana soon.

He pulled out a sheet of writing paper. His mother would want to know.

Dear Mom,

I watched for you all today. Hoped you would come and celebrate this milestone with me. I've worked hard and accomplished what I set out to do. Now I am ready to move on to the next phase. I guess if Dad's not interested in my graduation, then he's not interested in seeing me. So I'm not coming home on leave before I go to my new assignment.

But I will send you my address once I get there. I don't know if you receive my letters or not. Guess you aren't allowed to respond. Just hoping the silence is only Dad. Not you too. I love you both. Can't help it. I wish... Well, wishing won't change things.

I need to get ready for the Graduation Banquet. The ceremony is at ten tomorrow morning. In less than twenty-four hours I'll be a second lieutenant. It seems so strange. My new post is in North Carolina, at Fort Bragg. I'll write once I'm settled.

Your son,

Jimmy

He read through it one more time, making sure it said what he wanted. Then, after folding it, stuck it in the envelope and sealed it before he could change his mind. As an afterthought, he sent it in care of his uncle. They'd give Mom the letter. He'd address it to only her, so they shouldn't hand it off to his dad. He knocked on his wooden desk and added a stamp.

Ernie came back, rubbing his hair with his towel. "Better go 'fore there's no hot water."

Good idea.

The Graduation Banquet in Washington Hall at seven o'clock that evening, (civilian time or at nineteen hundred hours military time), required each graduate to attend in full regalia.

A few hours later, Jimmy and Ernie entered Washington Hall's Cadet Mess. Ernie's folks met them at the door and let them lead the way. After showing their tickets, they found their places at their banquet table gleaming with crystal and china and polished silver. This was dining at the finest level. If only his parents were here.

He made it through the five-course meal working to be charming and gallant, whatever that was. Ernie's folks had been so gracious. They deserved his best behavior. But once dinner was over and the Graduation Ball was about to start, he'd put in an appearance so no one would talk and then slip away. He had no date for the dance and no girl on his horizon to even stoke an interest.

An announcer entered the stage after the first couple of songs. Jimmy saw that as his cue to leave, but as he neared the door, whoever it was playing host introduced Ruth Etting to sing a couple of numbers. The crowd inside the ballroom exploded with applause and whistles as the lanky brunette walked out. "I am so honored to sing for you all tonight. This one is special for all our graduates." The orchestra gave an intro, and she began Irving Berlin's "The Song is Ended (But the Melody Lingers On)."

She may have been singing about a finished love affair, but the wistful tone fit his melancholy to a T. It was more than he could handle. He took his cue and left for the barracks.

The walk home led him past a few couples enjoying the bits of music floating from the ballroom, adding romance to their evening. If he had a girl, perhaps this trouble with his folks wouldn't be so difficult to swallow. But he'd kept his nose to his books, focused on his studies, and ended up ranked in the top twenty-five of the graduating class. Ernie was there too. Their friendship was so deep, they'd chosen many classes together. Even penned their senior paper as a joint effort—pass or fail, it would be as a team. When the two of them approached Colonel Langstrom about it, he'd been hesitant. But once he heard their outline, he encouraged their plan with the only extra provision to the assignment being he had to be able to tell that both had done equal work. They had. It would be nice to learn how they did on it, but that they were included in the graduation exercises told him they passed.

And tomorrow, he'd receive his officer's commission, his uniform, and butter bars—second lieutenant bars.

Lieutenant James R. Salem, an officer, and a gentleman. The Academy had taught him everything he needed, he only had to go into the world and apply it.

Should be easy, as long as he stayed away from Breadville and his father.

The next morning sunshine streamed through the window into his eyes as reveille sounded. Jimmy rolled over. Then it hit him.

"Ern, Ernie, it's today." He stretched a long leg out and gave his roommate's bed a push.

"I'm awake."

"When d'you get in last night?" Jimmy hopped up and grabbed his shaving kit.

"Around twenty-three hundred. Dad and Mom got tired. The time change helped, but Dad's so used to being up at the crack of dawn to milk that he always goes to bed early. Where d'you run off to? Surprised to find you already asleep when I got here."

He flipped his towel over his shoulder. "I didn't want to stand around and wasn't in a dancing mood. I slipped out while Ruth Etting was singing."

"What a surprise. They said she's working on Broadway right now so that's how they were able to get her. Mom nearly fainted. I think she knows all her songs from the radio."

"I'll be back." He shaved and showered and returned to dress for breakfast. His final meal as a cadet.

Weird to call the graduates Firsties when everything he did this morning reminded him it was the last time.

Afterward they changed into their dress uniforms and headed to where the Firsties would meet to cross the bridge and march to The Plain. Together, one final parade. Jimmy imagined a sky view looking down on a stream of white caps flowing with precisioned movements toward the pool of lawn where they would take their seats, listen to encouraging words, and finally toss those white caps in the air, never to wear it again. With that huge of a class, it was impossible to find your own. So the Firsties developed a tradition of writing messages inside. The administration allowed children in attendance to run to the field and choose a hat. Something simple could stir important dreams. His own dream came about after a West Point grad who'd fought in the Civil War spoke at his school. He was in fourth grade and still heard the sounds of battle that speaker described. Jimmy didn't know how, but at that moment he was certain, he would attend the academy.

Inside the cap he now wore, he'd penned his message "Keep dreaming. They can come true." He'd tried for profound, but that was his best.

If they'd been seated alphabetically, Ernest Wheaten would have been several rows behind James Salem. But as the powers that be designed them to sit according to their academic rank-ing, the friends were on the same row with only two classmates between them. They knew neither was the goat. It wasn't bad to be the goat—more than one general graduated last with his class

—and what do you call the last to be graduated from West Point? Lieutenant. Just like the first. But if a body wanted to prove to that body's father that he is worthy, it didn't pay to chance fate over being the goat.

The ceremony started. Jimmy listened intently to the speaker, hoping for some nugget of truth to carry him to his new post.

"At the academy, they taught you men strategies and practices to overcome obstacles, patterns and processes to plan your next move. But I'm here today to tell you it means nothing unless you are strong. I don't mean physically like General MacArthur meant when he said 'Every Cadet an Athlete.'

"No, I mean the strength that sustains in the worst of times, in the toughest of times. I pray to God that none of you will see another war. The Great War was the one to end all wars. I hope it keeps its word. But war or not, you are adults. There will be hard times and crisis and defeat.

"So how do you maintain your strength? With joy. Joy is your secret weapon. And only one joy will do. The joy of the Lord. That is your strength. Not happiness, joy. That quiet calm amid chaos that reminds you that all this is fleeting, but He holds it together in His hands. That rain or shine, God is still on His throne and He will work it out for your good and His glory.

"That is joy—knowing that you are intimate with that truth with every fiber of your being and living like it is. If you put joy at the top spot on your strategy list, you'll make it fine. I didn't say you would avoid pain or heartache, but you will make it. That is your strength. Go forth in joy and conquer your world."

Joy is the secret weapon? That wasn't the nugget he'd hoped for.

The superintendent began calling the Firsties for their diplomas. Soon after, their officer had everyone stand, caps on head. "Class of 1928, dismissed!" Caps flew into the air, and somehow Jimmy's sore heart soared a bit with them. He was graduated.

Ernie grabbed him in a bear hug and then pounded his back.

"We did it! We did it!" He dragged Jimmy off to find his folks who also had hugs for both guys.

"You still have things to do?" His mom wanted to keep them on the schedule.

"Yeah, Mom. We need to finish packing up our room, change into our new uniforms, and get our butter bars."

"Thanks again, Mrs. Wheaten, Mr. Wheaten. It was nice meeting you." Jimmy started to tip his hat but realized his head was bare. "Let's go. I want to get that pin."

"Me too." Ernie had one more hug for each parent, and then they ran to their barracks. Their gear was packed and ready. Five minutes later, they were in their new Class A's and searching for a ranking officer to pin on their second lieutenant bars.

Colonel Langstrom was the first they found, and he smiled at their request. "I am glad to run into you gentlemen. I've a bit of news. Your paper was outstanding. You are to be congratulated. Don't be surprised it if turns up elsewhere."

Ernie's forehead wrinkled as he glanced from the colonel to Jimmy and back.

"Why, sir?" Jimmy was as curious.

"This is my last semester here too. They've accepted me at the Army Industrial College, and I plan to take your paper with me. It's possible students there might be interested in discussing your theories."

He had no words. Jimmy's mouth worked but his brain couldn't push out a meaningful sound.

Ernie squeezed his shoulder. Hard. "Thank you, sir. That is splendid news. Thanks!"

When Jimmy glanced at him, Ernie's eyes were rounder than he ever thought they could be.

Colonel Langstrom busted into a laugh. "Now I figure out how to make you two speechless. Let's get these bars pinned so you can start behaving as second lieutenants."

04 July 1928

Fort Bragg, North Carolina

Second Lieutenant James Salem returned the salute from the infantry corporal who high-tailed it past on some important mission but knew he'd better acknowledge a superior officer before resuming his quest.

A part of Jimmy couldn't get used to all the saluting at him. He'd been well-schooled in the protocol, for sure. But this was the real world. Somehow, he feared it was a dream and he might wake to learn Dad was right.

He was to meet Ernie for dinner at the Officer's Club. Though they landed in different areas, they were stationed close, for which Jimmy was grateful. Ernie chose Army Air Corps at Pope Airfield next to where Jimmy picked Infantry at Fort Bragg. Just like in their paper. Still no word from Colonel Langstrom concerning that. It was a pipe dream, anyway.

Ernie arrived at the door seconds after Jimmy, and they entered together to find a table. It being a holiday, they hoped for good entertainment. The place wasn't crowded. They wrangled a spot near the stage and ordered the barbecue dinner with peach pie à la mode for dessert.

Before heading for the club, Jimmy had checked his mailbox. It was a shock to see he had mail. A part of him wanted to tear it open right away, but he waited. Only now, with Ernie there, he changed his mind and pulled out the envelope. "Found this in my box today. It's not my mom's handwriting so I'm a little nervous."

"Is it from Breadville?"

Jimmy nodded. "But Mom is the only person I gave my address to, so I haven't a clue."

"You never will unless you open it, sap."

"Fine." Jimmy slipped his finger under the flap and tore it

open. It revealed several pages covered in a feminine script. He read the first page and then passed it on to Ernie while he kept reading. At the end he handed over the last one and shook his head. "I had no idea my dad was so stubborn. Nor that Uncle Lyle was so…"

"Brotherly? Of course he would hand it to his brother. It's a good thing your cousin was there to retrieve it from the trash and watch for the next letter. At least you know what happened. And that it wasn't your mom."

Ernie was right. Uncle Lyle wouldn't have expected his own brother to keep mail from Jimmy's mother. His cousin Melanie said her dad was as shocked as anyone, but didn't want to get in the middle of things. Good ol' Mel. What was she now, thirteen? He shook his head. Guess he was lucky she was there when he delivered the letter.

"So, what will you do now? Your dad won't let your mom have any of your letters, and she doesn't know where to send mail to you." Ernie wasn't offering sympathy or commiserating. His questions inspired problem solving. Jimmy counted on him on for that.

"Guess I'll write to Mel and keep her informed in case she ever gets to talk to Mom alone. I don't think my Uncle will keep my letters from her. She said he didn't like what Dad did. I can only hope. At least it's something, and it solves the mystery."

Ernie nodded and handed back the letter as the stage curtains opened to a piano with pianist. Jimmy relaxed in his seat letting the patriotic music wash over him. Others had given up a lot more for their country. Why should he be different?

An announcer came next to introduce the singer for the evening. Valerie Beauregard. A nice southern name for sure. Then she walked out. A nice pretty southern girl. For sure. But when she opened her mouth to sing, he changed his mind. Nice. Beautiful. Angel. Wow.

Her first song was the same number Ruth Etting sang during

graduation weekend, "The Song Has Ended (But the Melody Lingers On)." Ruth had nothing on Miss Valerie Beauregard.

Jimmy hadn't been this affected by a girl in a long time—not since Sylvia McAllister his freshman year of high school, and then only until she started talking. She wouldn't shut up. He shivered at the memory of that close shave.

But this baby vamp had it all. Poise, beauty, and a voice sweet as dew drops on a spring morning. It was impossible to tell, her up on the stage and all, just how tall she stood. Plus her shoes had heels. But her dress showed off her long, lean figure with gams that went on forever. He couldn't take his eyes off her.

She sang another of Ruth Etting's hits, "Love Me or Leave Me," followed by a couple made popular by Helen Kane—"I Wanna Be Loved by You" and "That's My Weakness Now." To close, she leaned on the piano and sang the Gershwin brothers' "The Man I Love." Jimmy could have sworn she stared at him. It caused little tingles to run up his back, daring him to be the guy the song described.

He needed to meet this girl.

As she took her last bow, he stood searching for a way backstage.

"Where are you going?"

Jimmy startled. He'd forgotten Ernie sat at the same table. He ran his hand over his face and grinned. "To see her."

Ernie didn't stop him—probably could tell it wouldn't work. He shrugged. "Go get 'em tiger."

Jimmy winked and headed toward the side of the stage. He was only a couple yards away when she stepped through a door and ambled in his direction.

Was she coming his way? He smiled and did a little finger wave.

She tipped her head to the side, like she didn't understand something. "Did y—" Crash!

A busboy with a full tray of dishes plowed smack into her, dumping a pitcher of water down her front.

Jimmy rushed to her aid. "Oh, are you all right?"

The busboy lay on the floor, a gash on his arm.

She stemmed the blood with her scarf. "Can ya help him up? Maybe we'll find him a bandage in the office."

Jimmy got the poor guy—whose dusky skin turned rosier—on his feet while she kept pressure on the wound. She led the way down a short hall where she knocked on a door.

"Come in."

"I'm sorry to bother you, but do y'all have a first-aid kit?"

A captain Jimmy hadn't met rounded the desk. "Yeah, sure. Bring him in here. What happened?"

"He was loaded down, and I didn't see him when I stepped in his way." She took the fault, probably keeping the guy off report for carrying a load too large for the safety of the patrons. Through the whole incident, the busboy—a private on duty and assigned to the Officers Club—never said a word.

"Don't worry about it." It was then the captain noticed Jimmy who saluted. "Pulled you away from your meal, huh, Lieutenant?"

"No, sir. I was on my way to speak with the young lady when it happened." Now she'd know his plan. Would she still be willing? With her soaking dress and all? "Perhaps I should help the lady unless you need us?"

The captain shook his head. "I've got this. You two go on. Thanks for bringing him." They were dismissed.

Jimmy guided Miss Valerie Beauregard down the hall and toward the dining room. "I'm sorry about your dress, but wanted to tell you how much I enjoyed your singing."

She kept glancing in the office's direction. "That's sweet. Ya sure he'll be okay?"

"I'm sure. My name is Jimmy. Jimmy Salem." A thought struck him, and he acted before he could talk himself out of it. "May I give you a ride home? I've got a car."

They continued toward the front door as they spoke.

"Y'really don't need to—"

"Oh, no trouble. I'd be happy to escort you home. Good thing it's not winter, or you might freeze. Or does North Carolina get that cold? I've only been here a month." He held the door for her.

"A month? That's not long at all. The winters get colder, but I'm guessing not like where you're from. And really, y' don't need to—"

"Val, this guy bothering you?"

Jimmy glanced away from Miss Beauregard in time to see a middle-aged joe grab her by the arm and yank her behind him.

"What did you do to her? How'd she get all wet, and why is she bleeding?" The guy shoved Jimmy against the Officers Club wall as a crowd appeared.

She tried to pull the man away. "Uncle Teddy, stop. He did nothing. He was helping me. Teddy!"

"Is there a problem here, Lieutenant?"

Jimmy glanced over Uncle Teddy's shoulder to Ernie and a couple other officers. "No, no trouble here, right? *Uncle* Teddy?"

The fella let Miss Beauregard pull him back. But after a step he spun. "You army jerks are all alike. Well y' can keep your hands off my niece, even if she thinks you're only helping." He stormed off, his voice floating behind as he yelled at her. "Just get in the car." He turned the crank on the front and hopped in.

Jimmy exhaled and discovered he'd been holding his breath.

The others wandered away, but Ernie remained. "Did you at least learn where she lives?"

Jimmy shook his head. "No, but I will. Ernie, that's the girl I'm going to marry."

Saturday, 14 July 1928

Jimmy parked the Model A in front of the five-and-dime. He and Ernie put in together to buy the car. Jimmy had the afternoon free, but Ernie got called away on something else. The perfect time to cruise the town. Word had it on the base that Buster Keaton's recent film was a riot, so he figured why not?

Though not a large city by any means, Fayetteville was bigger than Breadville, for sure. It didn't take long to find the movie theater. The next showing was in an hour. No problem. There was that diner he spotted up the street. Bet he might grab a piece of pie.

The sign in the window advertised a soda named Cheerwine and suggested a Cheerwine float rather than a root beer float. He was game.

The bells on the door tinkled as he entered. He sat at the counter. A brunette at the rear booth called, "Be right there."

He shrugged and grabbed a menu from the holder. There might be something else worth trying, though that Cheerwine float sure sounded good.

"What can I get ya?"

A charge ran up his spine. He knew that voice. In fact, he'd been at the Officers Club every night since Independence Day hoping to hear it again. And now here she was. He lowered the menu. "Miss Beauregard?"

She stared at him a minute and then smiled. "I remember. You're Lieutenant Jimmy Salem. Been wanting to say how sorry I am about how Uncle Teddy behaved."

"No big deal. He was protecting you. How've you been?"

"Jake, just jake. So what can I get you?"

He smiled at her idiom. "Tell me about Cheerwine. What is it?"

"My favorite soda. Not wine, if that's what you're thinking. Nah, they call it that because of the color. But the taste is the elephant's eyebrows."

"You sold me. I'll take a Cheerwine float."

She tapped her pencil on the order pad and then tucked it behind her ear. "Okeydoke, be right back."

Jimmy put the menu away and glanced around the diner.

Business was slow. Beyond slow. More like dead. When did they close?

She returned with a mug filled with a couple scoops of vanilla ice cream and a dark-red liquid poured on top. A straw and long-handled spoon stuck out. It reminded him of a root beer float but for the color. "Don't be timid, try it." She watched as he used the straw to draw up a sip.

"Hey, this *is* delicious."

"Told ya. Well, gotta get back to work."

"What time are you off?"

"Why?" She stared, daring him to say the wrong thing.

"Just wondered if you might want to see *Steamboat Bill, Jr.* with me. It starts in about fifty minutes."

"Ya plan to take me to a petting pantry?"

His face grew fiery. "Oh, no, nothing like that. Thought you'd enjoy the picture."

She smiled. "Won't be off in time. Maybe another?"

"Sure, sure. Now that I know where you work, I might become a regular customer." He winked, and she chuckled. He loved her chuckle—warm, friendly, not forced.

"I've got some napkin holders to fill. Call me when you're ready to pay." She headed toward the kitchen.

At least they'd had more conversation than last time. And she didn't talk his ear off. In fact, he enjoyed hearing her, especially when she used slang. It went with her voice. Well, not her singing voice. That was symphonic. But her speaking with that bit of soft southern drawl was music to his ears.

He shook his head. Here he'd only seen her twice, and he was getting goofy. Imagining them setting up a household on base. She was the one. For sure.

After a glance at his wristwatch, he figured daydreaming time was over if he was going to make the picture. He slurped the last slurp through the straw and then spooned out the rest. Even if Miss Beauregard didn't work here, he'd crawl back for another one of these. "Ready."

She appeared faster than he expected. "I guess ya liked it. Fifteen cents."

"I did. Will definitely get more. Thanks for recommending it." He handed her a dime and a nickel.

"I could recommend other stuff on the menu. I'll show ya next time."

He liked how she said next time. "What if I come back? After the picture? I'll give you a ride home."

She shook her head. "I couldn't put ya out. Plus, ya don't need to tangle with Uncle Teddy. He'll be by to pick me up when he gets off work."

"Oh." Someone popped his happy balloon.

"But I'm glad ya stopped by so I could apologize." Her gaze made him want to hide behind his hands like a two-year-old. How did she turn him to jelly?

"Don't give it another thought. But do decide what I should order next time." He winked, hoping he appeared more suave than he felt.

"I'll do that. See ya around, Jimmy Salem."

"Yes you will, Valerie Beauregard." He gave her a brief wave and headed out the door. *Yes, you will for sure.* So now he had to answer an important question. How soon was too soon to return?

Forget that question. The real one he wanted answered was, how soon was too soon to propose?

To pre-order *Relentless Joy*, go here: https://www.amazon.com/dp/B08FX4QFH1 .